CRAWLERS

RAY GARTON

This book is dedicated to

Joe Parks

for years of friendship and movies.

Introduction

My childhood was made up primarily of books, movies, and TV. I think I came out of the womb a fan of horror and I began seeking out the genre and its cousins, science fiction and fantasy, as soon as I was capable. I was a good student, always did all of my homework, and did well in school, but when I got home, I went straight to the TV and fell into a world of *Batman* and *Ultraman* and monsters and ghosts and robots and dinosaurs and sword-fighting skeletons, a world in which anything from a tiny insect like an ant to the cuddliest bunny rabbit to the angriest woman could grow to gigantic sizes and menace a whole city or all of civilization. It was a world in which a scientist could put together the pieces of dead bodies to form a whole, functioning creature, and he could do it over and over in movie after movie; a world in which a reanimated dead guy who remains undead forever as long as he drinks blood sucked from the veins of the living does exactly that again and again in movie after movie.

The first half of the 1970s was a period in which made-for-TV movies on the three networks—that's all the TV there was at the time—began making dark movies, with the *ABC Movie of the Week* the leader of the pack. Most of them fell into the horror genre or at least landed on the fringes, but even those that weren't had grim stories and, like the horror movies, bleak endings in which love did not triumph, the bad guys won, and everybody died, endings that sometimes left me feeling utterly hopeless. It was in those TV movies, I think, that I began to see how storytelling could manipulate the emotions of the audience like a puppeteer tugging the strings of a marionette. Those TV movies had minuscule budgets, but they messed with our heads and emotions with the use of distorting camera lenses and bizarre angles, and especially with the help of some of the creepiest music I've ever heard.

Obviously, I was a TV junkie growing up. I could tell time by what was on TV and I memorized the listings at the beginning of every week. But at the same time, I was inhaling books. I read voraciously, not just in the horror genre but in all *kinds* of genres. But it was the horror novels and stories that always hit me the hardest. I was taught the art of horror by the best, writers like Richard Matheson, Rod Serling, William F. Nolan, Ray Bradbury, Stephen King, Peter Straub, Bari Wood, Robert R. McCammon, John Farris, Shirley Jackson, T.M. Wright, Richard Laymon, Flannery O'Connor, Thomas Tessier, Michael McDowell, and so many others. While TV and movies fired my imagination, I fell into books in a way that I could not fall into TV. There were no exciting but prepackaged images in silvery black and white or blood-drenched color, no special effects cheap or otherwise. There were only words on a page and all the rest took place inside my head. That kind of immersion is intoxicating and can be found, I think, only in books. I fell in love with it then and I'm still going back for more.

In one way or another, all of those books, movies, and TV shows have influenced my work and pieces of all of them show up scattered throughout. But occasionally, I write something that is a direct acknowledgment of one of those influences. *Crawlers* is such a novella. It is inspired by the many low-budget horror movies set in small, remote towns—most often in a desert, but in this case a mountain town—where everyone knows everyone else, and where something strange begins to happen. Whether the culprit is a giant spider or an alien invasion, the town is turned on its head by a supernatural menace that threatens not only the residents but the whole world.

I wrote it around the same time I wrote '*Nids*, which was an affectionate nod to giant spider movies. It was originally published as a hardcover edition in 2005 by Cemetery Dance Publications for members of their Collectors Club only, making it an extremely limited edition. Which brings me to the circumstances of writing this novella.

For the first decade of the new millennium, I was disabled by a bad hip that required a few operations and I spent all of that time on painkillers. Really good painkillers. The kind of painkillers that make you feel like the happiest person on earth for the first, oh, I don't know, year or so. After that they turn you into a zombie who goes from no mood at all to pissed the hell off in seconds. I was on them for almost ten years. Once I came out the other end of that, I began discovering stories and novellas that I had absolutely no memory of writing. Reading something you know you wrote but don't remember writing is a creepy experience.

I remembered writing *Crawlers*, but I did not remember the ending, which I found appalling. It was, in my estimation, an indigestible blend of horror with the treacly sensibilities of the late painter Thomas Kinkade. I want to claim that I don't know what I was thinking, but the fact is that I wasn't doing a lot of thinking at the time, and the result was an out-of-place happy ending that made little sense.

I have rectified that with this edition of *Crawlers* by giving the book a new ending more suited to the rest of the story and, I think, to our current times.

The story takes place in the fictional mountain town of Mount Crag, the home of my novellas *The Folks* and *The Folks 2: No Place Like Home*, although it is otherwise unrelated to those books.

I'm glad you're here, and I hope you enjoy the story.

Chapter One

1

"They fell out of the sky last night and landed right on my front lawn," Myra Henderson said. "And this mornin' they've bloomed into the prettiest things, don'tcha think?"

Naomi laughed. "I don't think any of the Leonid meteors landed on your lawn last night, Myra."

"Well, I suppose not. I didn't *see* 'em fall out of the sky, of course. But the spot of ground each was growin' out of is all black, like it's burnt, even though it's been raining. Just a little spot about the size of a quarter. I can show you, if you want. I figured maybe it was some of them meteors. I been hearin' people on the radio all mornin', they saw 'em come right through the clouds last night, close by. They're beautiful flowers, aren't they?"

They were, but when Naomi had first set eyes on them, she had thought they were artificial. They were so large and waxy and sturdy that they appeared to be plastic. Five of them stood on Myra's round Formica-topped kitchen table. She had dug up each flower and put it in a small green plastic pot, then put them on the table over which she had spread some newspapers. A few stray clumps of dirt were scattered over the newsprint.

The stems were thick, stiff, and brown at the bottom, but gradually eased from brown to green on the way up. Each stem had stout brown thorns that grew upward, not unlike the thorns on a rose's stem. The flowers had eight petals of deep burgundy about six or seven inches in length. The petals were narrow in width, but thick and muscular with a polished shine. Each petal grew up from the center of the flower at an angle, then curled acutely downward at the halfway mark and tapered to a sharp, curved, brown thorn at the tip. The center of each flower was round and fat in the middle, beaded and black with a shimmering iridescent sheen.

Naomi bent over and smelled one of the flowers, but it had no scent. "I've never seen anything like them," she said.

"Neither have I. I couldn't find 'em in any of my gardening books. There's more of 'em out there, lots more, they're *every*where. And all of a sudden, too. They weren't there yesterday. I never saw 'em before in my life and today, just like that, they're everywhere."

Naomi had not noticed any of the flowers on her way in, but then she had been too preoccupied with thoughts of her classes to look for them.

Myra's cat hopped up on the table and rubbed against Naomi. He was black, gray, and white, with a white face and a strip of black just under his nose, like a mustache.

Naomi stroked the cat and said, "Hey, Groucho." The cat arched his back and purred.

"What are you up to this morning, honey?" Myra said.

"I just got back from classes in Iron Falls and I need to do a little grocery shopping. I thought I'd drop by here first and see if you need anything at the store."

"Oh, you're such a sweetie." Myra turned and limped over to the square corkboard mounted on the wall above her telephone. Postcards and photographs and newspaper clippings were fastened to the cork with colorful push pins.

At seventy-four, Myra Henderson was spry in spirit, but had been hobbled by arthritis, particularly in her hips. Not so long ago, she had been active and was seldom home, but as the arthritis worsened she had become more housebound. Myra had been Grandma's best friend. Since Grandma's death six years ago, Naomi dropped by now and then to see if there was anything she could do for her.

Myra said, "I made a list, and I think I stuck it up—yep, here it is." She pulled a red pin from the board and took down a slip of lavender paper.

On the counter beside an ancient Raggedy Ann and Andy cookie jar stood an old black-and-silver AM radio tuned to an Iron Falls news/talk station. It was the same station Naomi had been listening to on her drive back to Mount Crag from Iron Falls. Callers were discussing the previous night's Leonid meteor shower.

Forecasters had predicted the shower would be the most vivid in a century, and likely would not be as spectacular for another hundred years. Naomi had gone out on her front porch to see it, but it had been raining for two days and nights straight, and the shower had been hidden behind the heavy cloud cover. She had not wasted any time on the porch and had gone straight back inside.

Myra smiled as she limped back across the small, cozy kitchen and handed Naomi the list. "Are you gonna go to the Save-King and see your honey?"

"Of course. I'd feel like a traitor if I shopped at Safeway." Naomi's boyfriend Chuck was manager of the Save-King supermarket. She usually timed her shopping trips to coincide with Chuck's breaks, but she would be way off this morning.

"You want me to give you some cash now?" Myra said.

"No, we can work that out when I get back."

"Well, you know all the brands I buy. Because you're such a sweetie to remember, that's why."

Naomi smiled. "I have to stop at the diner and get my paycheck, then deposit it at the bank. Then I'll come straight back here from the supermarket."

Myra said, "I ain't goin' nowhere."

2

Naomi DiRisio had lived all of her twenty-three years in the small mountain town of Mount Crag. She had attended Mount Crag Elementary and Middle Schools, then went just down the street to graduate from Thomas Jefferson High School. In all that time, she had never seen a single flower like those Myra had dug up in her front yard. Now, they were everywhere she looked as she got into her Ford Escape XLS in front of Myra's house.

Naomi's grandfather had founded DiRisio Lumber, a thriving lumberyard located between Mount Crag and Iron Falls, a city twenty-five miles to the east. The company had been passed on to her father, Paul. Naomi's mother, Laura, a nurse, had been working at Iron Falls Medical Center for a dozen years when Paul died of a massive coronary during Naomi's sophomore year in high school. With no one to fill his shoes, Laura had quit her job and briefly tried to run the business, but had found it too daunting a task. She had sold the lumberyard and invested the money well.

Naomi had attended Iron Falls Community College for two years, but dropped out when she was unable decide what she wanted to do with her life. She had worked for three years at the Pinwheel Day Care Center in Iron Falls and for a time had toyed with the possibility of becoming a teacher, but the idea had never caught fire.

Then she had befriended a massage therapist who regularly treated both Laura and Myra. When she saw how much they benefitted from it, she had become interested in going into massage therapy herself. She had quit her job at Pinwheel last summer and enrolled in the Granite River Institute of Massage Therapy in Iron Falls, where she was studying to get her license. Money was not a big concern; on top of the money from the sale of DiRisio Lumber, with which her mother was quite generous, Grandma had left Naomi a handsome inheritance, all of which she had invested conservatively. But to keep from becoming idle while studying for her license, Naomi had gotten a part-time job at the Pantry Shelf diner in Mount Crag. Her boss, Carrie Lodge, had scheduled her to work around her classes at the institute.

Naomi lived in what was originally a guest house behind the rambling Victorian in which she had grown up. When Grandma moved in, it stopped being a guest house and became Grandma's place. She had insisted that Naomi take the place when she was gone, and her mother, Laura, had agreed. The house gave her all the privacy she needed and still allowed her to be close by for her mother, who had an unpredictable heart condition.

Bart Henderson had been caretaker of the Green Hills Cemetery in Mount Crag for decades, and the house in which Myra now lived alone was on a hill overlooking the rear of the graveyard. As Naomi drove back down the hill along the narrow gravel road called Henderson Way—it was really nothing more than a long driveway—she saw the tall burgundy flowers growing on both sides. They had even sprouted up in the vast expanse of lawn at the foot of the hill, among the rows of gravestones. They were everywhere. She ran over a few that stood in the middle of the road on her way to Yardley Street, which led to Main Street and into Mount Crag.

Naomi turned on the radio. A male caller said, "I don't care what the experts say, I saw a bunch of them shoot through the clouds late last night. They was close, too. They couldn't've landed very far from here."

"And where are you, sir?" the host said. His name was Larry Baker and he always sounded upbeat, with an artificial smile in his baritone voice.

"I'm in Iron Falls, and I saw them go down west of here, toward Mount Crag."

"We haven't had any reports of meteors striking anywhere in the area," Baker said, "but I've been getting calls all morning about this, even though our meteorologist tells us the meteors would burn out while entering the atmosphere and wouldn't—"

"Yeah, I know, I heard, but that's what I saw. Maybe it wasn't meteors, but it was sure *somethin'*."

"Thanks for calling. It's ten-eighteen in the a.m. and it's a gloomy, rainy Friday out there. But the weatherman says it'll all start clearing up later today and we'll have sunshine for the weekend. The community calendar is coming up—"

Naomi switched to FM and found a station playing something by Norah Jones.

The wipers swept over the windshield at high speed to keep up with the rainfall as she turned onto Main Street and drove past the park into town. After parking at the curb in front of the hardware store, she got out and opened her umbrella, then hurried across the street to the Pantry Shelf.

Inside, she collapsed her umbrella and leaned it against the wall by the coat rack, where there were already a few other umbrellas on the plastic mat. The diner was warm and smelled of eggs and bacon. The coffee cups were neatly turned over at each empty seat along the counter and at the empty booths, waiting to be filled for the next newly-seated customer, the way Carrie's father had done it since he first opened the place. She smiled as Naomi stepped behind the counter, took two breakfast plates from the order window, and handed them to her.

"Your check's on the counter by the register, hon," Carrie said. "You want some coffee?"

"No, thanks," Naomi said. "I've gotta run."

Carrie took the plates to Mrs. Fridley and Mrs. Sturgis, two middle-aged sisters and married mothers, who were seated at their usual front-window booth with cups of coffee, browsing the sales flyers in the *Iron Falls Sentinel*. They met at the diner every Friday morning for brunch before going shopping. Naomi had worked on Friday mornings last semester and used to wait on them regularly. Mrs. Fridley, a stout woman with short brown hair, always had the huevos rancheros, and the slender but rather frumpy Mrs. Sturgis, with shoulder-length dark-blonde hair and wire-framed glasses, always ordered the Pantry Scramble. Mrs. Sturgis saw Naomi and smiled, waggled her fingers at her. Naomi smiled and waved back.

"Where's Maureen?" Naomi said. Maureen was the waitress scheduled to work that morning.

Coming back from the table, Carrie said, "Home with the flu. And I don't have a dishwasher. Rolly hasn't come in and he hasn't called. I called Vince and he said he'd come in, but he hasn't gotten here yet. I'm on my own this morning. Until Ruth comes in at noon."

Carrie was thirty-three, a petite woman with long chestnut hair she kept in a bun while she worked. Her blue Pantry Shelf smock covered a green sweatshirt and jeans. She had deep parentheses flanking her mouth, probably because she was always smiling. At the moment, she looked exhausted, and it was not even noon yet.

Naomi went to the register at the front end of the counter and found her paycheck in a plain white business envelope with her name written on it in Carrie's neat script. She put it in her purse.

"I've got to run an errand," Naomi said, "but when I'm done, I'll check back with you. If nobody's come in by then, I'll give you a hand."

Carrie smiled and said, "Thanks for offering so I wouldn't have to ask. I'd sure appreciate it, Naomi."

There was a man seated at the other end of the counter whom Naomi had never seen in the diner before. He wore a dark-gray suit and sat with his face buried in the newspaper.

"Nowmi!"

She turned to the order window where Gustav, the chef, grinned at her as he put both ham-like hands flat on the chrome counter. An upper front tooth capped with silver glimmered in his smile.

"Hey, Gustav, how's it going?"

"Eet goes, eet goes." He was an enormous man with a walrus mustache covered by a black net that stretched around the back of his head. He was completely bald beneath his cap and spoke with a heavy Hungarian accent. He rubbed the back of his neck. "My neck—ees killing me. When you be finished with school so you can massage my neck?"

Naomi laughed. "I've got a while to go, Gustav." She turned to Carrie. "I'll give you a call."

"Do that. And thanks."

She got her umbrella. On her way out, Officer Perry Milner came in wearing a raincoat. He held the door open for her.

"Thank you, Officer," Naomi said as she went outside. She headed for the bank.

3

"Morning, Perry," Carrie said.

Perry put his raincoat and plastic-covered cap on the rack and went to the coffee counter. "How about a cup of coffee and a bacon-and-egg sandwich to go," he said as he took a seat. He was tall and had thick red hair and a cluster of freckles on his forehead, with a midsection that was starting to thicken.

Carrie jotted down the order and put the ticket on the carousel in the order window, spun it half a revolution. "Did you miss breakfast this morning, Perry?"

"Suzy's got the flu," he said. "She wanted to get up and cook for us, but I told her to stay in bed. I made breakfast for the kids, but didn't have time to make any for myself. Tell you the truth, I'm lucky I didn't burn the kitchen down feeding them. So I'm starving."

"That flu's going around. Maureen's got it, and Lionel over at the drugstore's home with it, too. I've doubled up on my vitamin C. I don't even have a dishwasher this morning. I don't suppose you'd be interested in helping me out by washing some dishes, would you, Perry?"

He laughed. "I think my superiors would frown on that."

"Mushroom omelet," Gustav said at the order window.

Carrie turned and picked it up and Gustav gave her a twitch of his mustache.

He still looked the same as he had the first time Carrie had laid eyes on him when she was a little girl. He was a bear of a man, six-and-a-half feet tall and pushing three hundred pounds. Age had done little more than put bags beneath his eyes and add gray hairs to his bushy black mustache.

Carrie's father, Harold Lodge—Dutch to all his friends—had bought the place when it was a little Chinese restaurant that kept getting closed for health violations. He had cleaned it up, and Gustav had been the first employee hired. That had been before Carrie was born, back when Gustav was a young man of nineteen. Carrie's mother had decorated the diner simply, in cheerful blues and yellows. In photographs of its early days it had looked nearly bare compared to its current clutter. There had been a shelf on the back wall on which Carrie's mother had put a few small knickknacks. Then Dutch had come across a large ceramic Holstein cow that he was, for one reason or another, very fond of, and he put it in the center of the shelf. After that, people began giving Dutch Holsteins of all kinds—Holstein salt-and-pepper shakers, Holstein mugs, Holstein napkin holders, a Holstein music box, and just plain Holsteins made of plastic, rubber, plaster, glass, and even carved from wood. Now, there was a shelf high on each wall covered with Holsteins. There were framed photographs and paintings of Holsteins on the walls. The diner was cluttered with the cows. Every now and then, regular customers still presented Carrie with some new Holstein gift to add to the collection.

She had grown up in the diner. It had felt as much like home as the house she had shared with her parents and brother George. Ten years ago, her father had been diagnosed with lung cancer. She had taken the diner over while he endured the grueling treatments. They had behaved as if it was just a temporary arrangement, but they knew better. He had never returned to the diner to work. By then, George, a successful attorney, had married and moved to Spokane, Washington, so his wife could be close to her family. He flew home to be with Dutch during his final weeks. After Dutch died, Carrie's mother Alice had moved in with Carrie to help take care of Robby while Carrie managed the diner.

At first, Carrie had been doubtful about the arrangement. Her mother had a way of driving her crazy with little throwaway remarks about the choices she had made in her life, comments that sometimes started unpleasant arguments. Alice, for example, had disapproved of Wyatt, Carrie's ex-husband, who had proven her right by running off with an Iron Falls stripper when Robby was still a baby. Alice still brought up that particular mistake now and then. The situation was made worse when Alice drank, something she had been doing with increasing regularity before Dutch's death, which only increased significantly afterward. But after moving in, she had surprised Carrie by keeping her comments and observations to herself most of the time. A remark slipped out every now and then when she had a glass of wine too many, but even her drinking decreased after she moved in with them. She sometimes had a drink or two late at night when she could not sleep, but no more than that. They got along much better than Carrie had expected, and Robby loved his grandma. Good thing, too, because she would not know what to do without Alice there to take care of him while she worked.

She took the mushroom omelet to a man at the other table by the front window, then returned to the counter. A man sat at the end of the counter opposite the register looking as sad and distraught as he looked soft and lumpy. He wore a dark-gray suit and red-and-black tie but looked rumpled, as if perhaps he had slept in it. He kept checking his watch every few minutes as he made his way through the newspaper distractedly, then set it aside. He had finished his breakfast and she had taken his plate, but he lingered, drinking coffee, and staring at the countertop. As she cleared away a coffee cup and water glass left by a customer a few seats down the counter, she smiled and said, "Can I get you anything else, sir?"

"A little more coffee, please."

As Carrie filled the man's cup, Pete shuffled into the diner. She wiped the counter down, turned the coffee cup over, and smiled at him. "Morning, Pete. What've you got there?"

He carried a tall burgundy flower in a small ceramic pot. "I brought you a flower," he said as he put it on the counter. He took off his overcoat, shuffled over and hung it on the coat rack, leaned his umbrella against the wall, then sat at the counter between Perry and the gray suit.

Carrie poured a cup of coffee for Pete and looked the flower over. "That's for me? Thank you, Pete. That's awful nice of you."

"I thought it was purdy so I potted it for you." He sprinkled some sugar into his coffee.

Pete was a small, wiry man, a Vietnam vet with a glass eye that had a dozen stories behind it. A widower at seventy-one, he came into the diner every morning and sat for a couple of hours over coffee and an English muffin or a cinnamon roll while he read the paper. He was, in fact, one of the few who still read the daily paper that was always at the end of the coffee counter. Pete often said, "When you get to my age, you don't need a lot of sleep." That was why he listened to late-night radio and usually came to breakfast with news of some crazy theory discussed the night before—the government-alien conspiracy, CIA mind control tactics, Satanic cults made up of ultra-rich elitists, that sort of thing. His face was a leathery webwork of deep wrinkles, and he spoke loudly because he was deaf in his left ear and losing the hearing in his right. Dutch had told Carrie that Pete was the diner's very first customer.

"Ever seen a flower like that before?" Pete said.

Carrie frowned as she looked at it closely. "No, I can't say that I have. It's so pretty, it almost doesn't look real. It looks like some of the plastic flowers they sell at the dollar store."

"Yeah, that's what I thought, but there it was, growin' right beside my front steps, just outside the trailer."

"I saw a bunch of those in front of the station this morning," Perry said with a slight frown. "I know they weren't there yesterday."

"They're everywhere now," Pete said.

Carrie said, "Really? I didn't see them, but it was still dark when I came in this morning. You want the pot back, Pete?"

"Aw, no, you can have that old thing. I was keepin' screws and washers in it till I found that flower this morning. I woulda brought you more if I had somethin' else to put 'em in. They're all over the place out there. You might want to take it over to the nursery and see if they know what it is. Maybe they know how to take care of it."

"I might do that. Thank you, Pete. That was sweet of you."

"Well, you know you're m'honey." He chuckled before sipping his coffee. "Where's the paper?"

The man in the suit shoved the newspaper and it slid down the counter to Pete, who thanked him.

He unfolded and opened the paper noisily until he found an article he wanted to read, then he folded it backward and then in half. But he did not read the article. He looked at the page as he said to no one in particular, "Listened to a former NASA worker on the radio last night. He talked about the secret space program we've got going. Anybody listen to that?" He lifted his head and looked around.

"You know I don't listen to that stuff, Pete," Carrie said. "There's plenty of real stuff to be scared about without listening to those shows."

"Oh, you're right there, Carrie, no doubt about that. But they're entertaining as hell, those shows. I get a big kick out of them."

He always said that, absolving himself of any real attachment to the theories discussed into the wee hours, but Carrie knew he fully believed most of them. A trucker passing through town had come in one morning for breakfast a couple of weeks ago and struck up a conversation with Pete. He was a like-minded fan of late-night radio who listened to the same radio programs as Pete. Before long, they were fervently engaged in a conversation about what kind of deal the U.S. government might have made with the aliens that crashed in Roswell back in 1947 and how it might be connected to the massively screwed-up world they found themselves living in today. Pete was a believer, but he only let it show when he was in the company of another believer.

"Anyways, this guy says we've got off-world military bases," Pete said. "Out in space. We're fighting aliens. There are good ones and bad ones, and we're fighting the bad ones with the good ones."

"I'm sure if we're fighting them, they must be the bad ones."

Her sarcasm was not lost on Pete, who smirked and said, "Yeah, I know, you think I'm nuts. But you never know. It's not like our country hasn't been up to some pretty weird shit before that it's tried to keep secret."

"If he's telling the truth, they're not doing a very good job of keeping *that* secret. Why isn't he floating in a river or buried in a landfill by now?"

"Oh, who knows. Maybe he's just fulla crap. Or maybe they've been letting information leak out here and there over the years, gradually preparing us for the big one, and he's one of the leaks."

"The big one?"

"Yeah, the big reveal. That we're not alone and aliens have been among us for a long time. Or some shit like that."

"Sandwich," Gustav said at the order window.

Carrie put the flower beside the cash register, bagged Perry's sandwich with a few napkins, poured coffee into a Styrofoam cup and put a lid on it.

Perry stood and went to the register, took his wallet from his back pocket, and handed Carrie a twenty-dollar bill. "I'd sure appreciate it if you'd order up some sunshine for me, Carrie."

"It's coming up," she said as she made change. "The weatherman says this rain is supposed to clear up later in the afternoon."

"Let's hope so." He went over to the rack and put on his raincoat and cap. Dropping a tip on the counter, he snatched up his bag and coffee and said, "See you all later," on his way out.

4

Lucas Rowland had finished his breakfast some time ago but remained at the counter. It felt like he had been in the diner for hours, but he had been sitting there for only an hour and forty minutes. He felt bloated and jittery from all the coffee he had drunk and half-deaf from the ringing in his ears, probably due to lack of sleep and elevated blood pressure from stress. He had read the newspaper from front page to back, although he had not absorbed a word of it. His eyes had passed over the newsprint blindly while he imagined his wife in bed with another man. He never saw the man's face in his imagination, only his back as he humped away on top of Nancy in the bed Lucas had shared with her for over eighteen years, the bed in which they had conceived their second child and had made love…how many times?

He had never been inside the diner before, although he drove past it almost every day. He looked around at all the

Holstein cows on the shelves, but his mind barely registered them.

Lucas wondered if they had started yet, if they were going at it somewhere in the house at that very moment. He looked at his watch, something he had been doing every few minutes since he had arrived and ordered a Denver omelette. His watch was a few minutes behind the Holstein clock on the wall, and he wondered which was correct. Most of his breakfast seemed to have settled in a soggy lump halfway to his stomach. He took a roll of Tums from the pocket of his suit coat and popped one in his mouth. The crunch was loud in his head as he chewed it, but not loud enough to obliterate Nancy's cries of pleasure in his imagination.

He had no hard proof, or he would have confronted her with it. He had only suspicions and gut feelings. But he was not entirely sure he trusted those, so he had decided to see for himself. He had arranged to have the day off, but had left the house that morning and led Nancy to believe he was going to work as always. In fact, he had left a little early, skipping breakfast, but he had come instead to the diner.

They had married young; Nancy had just graduated from high school the year before and Lucas was a sophomore in college. She had gotten pregnant, but he had *wanted* to marry her. He had surprised himself by how very *much* he wanted to marry her. But he had not expected her to say yes, and when she had, it rendered him speechless.

They had met when he had done some tutoring at the library the previous summer and she had come in for help. She had been getting Bs and Cs in everything but her math classes and wanted to improve for her senior year. The relationship had come out of nowhere and so stunned Lucas that he did not even tell his friends about it for nearly a month. He was afraid it was not going to last, or it would turn out that she was doing it on a bet.

Nancy Thalman was a beautiful and popular girl, a *cheerleader*, for crying out loud. They had gone to Thomas Jefferson together a year apart, but they had not spoken to each other once in all that time because they hung with different crowds, lived in different worlds. Lucas had spent his time with the math geeks and hardly anyone outside that small crowd even knew he existed at school. But something had happened that summer that made all of that irrelevant, something he still could not put his finger on. The next thing he knew, they were married with a baby, and then another baby.

Now this. Lucas was willing to accept his share of the responsibility for this affair, but he would by no means take full blame. He had let things slide over the last few years and had come to take her for granted. When was the last time he had left her a sweet little note in the kitchen, or surprised her with a bouquet of flowers, or served her breakfast in bed on a Sunday? He used to do those things. They usually made love on the weekends, but it was mostly by rote. Things had gotten stale and he knew that was as much his fault as hers. But he had never been unfaithful to her. There had been a couple of opportunities, surprisingly enough, but neither of them could have held a candle to Nancy and were hardly tempting.

When had his insecurities worn off? When had the fear that Nancy would come to her senses and realize she had made a terrible mistake in marrying him gone away? When had his fears of inadequacy become feelings of complacency? He had become too comfortable in the marriage, that was part of the problem. He had allowed himself to forget that he was a math geek married to a goddamned *cheerleader*, for crying out loud.

He was a grown-up math geek now, a C.P.A. who was steadily climbing the ladder at the accounting firm of Burbeck and Schwartz in Iron Falls. He had developed a bit of a belly in his middle age. Nancy had gained some weight, too, but in all the right places, and it only made her more luscious. Lucas's belly only made him more Homer Simpsonish.

But she had lost weight lately and started working out regularly. She had cut her long blonde hair and wore it short and curly now. Lucas had found a sock in the bedroom that matched none of his. She was always smiling now, as if at an amusing secret. And how many whispered phone calls had he walked in on? He had even listened outside the kitchen doorway a couple of times, but had been unable to understand what she was saying. Then, when he walked in, she suddenly started speaking in her normal voice and said, "Okay, Becky, well, then, I'll talk to you later," and hung up. He knew she was not talking to her friend Becky, or her friend Sharon, or any of her other friends. When did she ever whisper to them? Usually when she was on the phone with her friends, he could hear her laughing through the whole house.

The kids were grown up now, teenagers with lives of their own. Derek was eighteen and attending college in Iron Falls and Cynthia would be seventeen next month. They did not need her at home as much as they used to, so Nancy had found someone to fill the gap. But who? Was it someone Lucas knew? He hoped not.

He got up and took his bill to the register, paid it, and put on his overcoat. He had left his umbrella in the car because he felt too miserable to hold it up. Hands buried in his coat pockets, he walked down the sidewalk to a sign that read PARKING IN REAR with an arrow painted on the bottom that pointed down an alley beside the building. He walked down the alley to the small parking lot behind the restaurant where he had parked his Taurus. He drove out of the lot and went up Main Street.

They lived near the park in a nice neighborhood overlooking the Granite River. He drove into the park, found a parking spot, got out, and locked his car. He would walk to his house. Through the park, he knew a way to the back yard so he could sneak up on the house from behind. They would not see or hear him coming.

5

After depositing her check at the bank, Naomi went to Save-King and picked up the things she needed, checked off the items on Myra's list, then got in line at one of the registers. She saw Chuck at the eastern end of the store. He looked busy, walking fast with his back straight. He wore the uniform of the Save-King manager: white shirt, dark-red tie, and black pants, with a red-and-white Save-King name tag on his breast pocket that identified him as General Manager. He was twenty-five, tall, with thick dark-blond hair and, in spite of his lean body, a round face. His upper lip had been scarred by a cleft palette that had been surgically repaired when he was very young. He was still quite self-conscious about the scar, which had made him the butt of a lot of cruel jokes while growing up, but Naomi thought it added character and distinction to his boyish face.

They had met there at the store one day last summer as she was on her way out with a bag of groceries. He had sheepishly said hello, introduced himself, and offered to help her out with the bag, but she had politely declined. She had been in a hurry at the time, but he kept returning to her thoughts. When she was next in the store, she had approached him and started a conversation. The next time, he had asked her to the Granite County Fair. He had been so shy and quiet on that date that she was not surprised to learn later that he had rehearsed for weeks

19

before finally mustering the courage to approach her in the store. They had been together ever since.

After making her purchase—she had Myra's groceries rung up on a separate receipt—she put the bags in her cart and pushed it over to the florist department, which took up the southeastern corner of the store. It smelled of roses and gardenias and was decorated as if for a party with ribbons and shiny Mylar balloons. Chuck was there talking to Denise Robillard, the florist, and Hattie Tucker, the mayor's wife and a local busybody. Mrs. Tucker was in her fifties, tall and rail-thin, and as usual, she wore a lot of makeup and was dressed as if she were on her way to church. She held in her arms a cardboard flat with three of the tall burgundy flowers standing in recycled cardboard pots.

When he saw Naomi, Chuck's face lit up and he reached out and took her hand. "Hey, sweetie," he said. He gave her a brief kiss on the lips.

Naomi nodded toward the flowers and said, "Myra dug up five of those and brought them in the house."

Mrs. Tucker said, "They're all over the place. I've never seen anything like them and thought I'd bring them in to see if Denise knows what they are."

"I'm sorry, but I don't," Denise said. "May I?" She took the flat from Mrs. Tucker, carried it over to the counter, and set it down. Her brow furrowed and she squinted slightly as she inspected them, smelled them.

"These are weird flowers," she said, still frowning, "and I have absolutely no idea what they are."

In her late thirties and stout, with auburn hair cut short, Denise was single-handedly responsible for Save-King's florist counter, and Chuck had said it was the store's most successful and smoothest-running department. Denise seemed to live there. Naomi could not remember ever seeing her outside the store and wondered what she did in her spare time.

"I suppose I could take them to the nursery," Mrs. Tucker said, "but I don't really have the time to go over there right now. Do you mind if I leave them with you, Denise?"

"Not at all," Denise said, still staring at the flowers with a creased forehead. "I'll crack open my books and see if I can identify them. Donald and Fanny from the nursery shop here, and if they come in, I'll see what they think of them."

"You're a dear," Mrs. Tucker said. "Today is Carol Raimey's birthday. You know, the head librarian over at the library, and some of the girls and I are putting together a little party for her around noon, and I'm in charge of the cake. I've come here to pick it up at the bakery." She tilted her head forward and lowered her voice. "Carol's teenage daughter Cathy is pregnant, you know, which is a *terrible* embarrassment for poor Carol. And her husband is unemployed, you know." She curled her fingers around an imaginary glass and tipped it up at her lips to mimic drinking. "She needs all the support she can get right now."

Denise said, "Do you want these back?"

"Oh, goodness, no. They're suddenly *everywhere,* so I can get others easily enough." She turned to Chuck. "How are your parents, Chuck? Are they well?"

He nodded. "They're fine. Dad's anxious to do some pheasant hunting. We're going out this weekend."

"Well, that's nice. Please tell them I said hello, would you do that for me?" She turned to Naomi. "And please, give my best to Myra Henderson. I hardly ever see her anymore. Is she well?"

"Her arthritis keeps her inside a lot these days," Naomi said.

"Does she ever hear from her son and daughter? Oh, what about her daughter, did she ever get remarried?"

As they talked, Denise closely inspected the flowers. "Mrs. Tucker, are you sure these flowers weren't there yesterday? There was no sign of them at all?"

"I've never seen them before, ever. This morning, they're everywhere I look. They're the prettiest things, if a little odd. They almost don't look *real*. But they certainly weren't there before this morning."

"Myra said the same thing," Naomi said. "They just popped up all of a sudden, out of nowhere. I know I've never seen them before today." She turned to Mrs. Tucker. "Myra said something else. Did you happen to notice if the ground around the flowers was—"

"It was black!" Mrs. Tucker said. "It looked as if it had been burnt, or something. The strangest thing."

Naomi frowned as she turned to Denise. "Have you ever heard of anything like that before?"

"Nope, afraid not," Denise said. "And I haven't heard of flowers showing up everywhere overnight, either. It almost sounds like some kind of prank." She looked at Chuck. "There aren't any new florists or nurseries opening up around here, are there?"

"You think it's a publicity stunt?" he said.

Denise shrugged. "It crossed my mind."

"Well, I *must* run," Mrs. Tucker said. "Denise, please give me a call if you manage to identify them, would you?" She turned and hurried toward the bakery at the other end of the store.

Chuck said quietly, "If she doesn't manage to find any gossip here in the store, do you think she makes it up in the car?"

Naomi and Denise laughed, but Denise's was abrupt. She frowned again, distracted by the flowers.

Naomi said to Chuck, "Are we still on for dinner tonight?"

"You bet. Mom's making her famous stew. Perfect weather for it."

"By the way," she said, pointing at the flowers on the counter, "if you bring me flowers, *those* won't count because they're everywhere."

Chuck laughed.

"Do you have time to walk me out to my car?" she said.

"Not today. The owner is coming in this morning. He could walk in any minute, and I need to make sure everything's ship-shape."

"Aye-aye, sir." She kissed him again. "I'll see you tonight, then." She pushed her cart of groceries out of the store.

6

Denise Robillard snapped a picture of the flowers, went to the desk in her office, and entered the photo into Google Image Search. All that came up were artificial flowers that looked as plastic as the one in her picture.

She took a large, fat book off a shelf on the wall, put it on her desk, and paged through it while standing, searching for something that resembled the three tall burgundy flowers in the flat on the counter.

She hefted the book out of the office and put it on the counter beside the flat. Mrs. Tucker had left and no one was waiting for service. She paged through the book a while longer, then stood up straight to examine the flowers again. She gasped and quickly looked down at the floor around her feet. Searching, she walked around to the front of the counter, looked around at the nearby shoppers, then at the flowers again as her frown grew even deeper.

The three tall, thorny stems were bare at the top. The eight-petaled flowers were gone.

Chapter Two

1

Naomi hugged a grocery bag with one arm, and held a plastic bag in her other hand, with her purse slung over her shoulder as she hurried up the front walk to Myra's door. The flowers were everywhere. They were in Myra's front lawn, where five small holes had been dug, each with a pile of muddy earth beside it. There were many more outside the split-rail redwood fence that surrounded the front yard. They grew along the road between the grocery store and Myra's house. *Everywhere.*

She had not brought her umbrella from the car, and by the time she reached the front door, the baggy brown-and-tan wool sweater and blue jeans she wore were mostly soaked. She opened the screen door and wiped her feet on the mat.

"I'm here," she said as she stepped into the house. She turned and closed the door. A few ropes of her long black hair were stuck to her face, and she brushed them aside as she went past the archway that led to the living room, down the hall, and into the kitchen.

The radio was silent. Naomi put the bag on the counter and dropped her keys beside it. "Myra?" When she spotted the flowers, she released a breathy, "Oh."

Each of the five flowers appeared to have been snipped off the stem. Naomi looked all around the kitchen for them but they were not there.

"Myra?" she called again.

Naomi decided she was probably in the bathroom. She took the milk and Egg Beaters from the bag and put them in the refrigerator, then left the kitchen and went farther down the hall. As she neared the bathroom, she heard a mewling sound coming from behind the closed door.

She thought, at first, the sound was being made by Groucho. Sometimes the cat sat on windowsills and became deeply absorbed in watching squirrels or other cats as they wandered in and out of the yard outside. As he watched them, Groucho often made a small mewling sound, and that was what Naomi thought she had heard at first.

But this mewling sound formed words: "Oh, Jesus, dear Jesus, oh, God, oh Jesus…"

Naomi took the last few steps to the bathroom. "Myra? Are you all right?"

"What? Who's that?" Myra's trembling voice was high and frail.

Panic made words tumble out of Naomi's mouth in a rush as she rattled the locked doorknob: "What's the matter? What's wrong? Let me in, Myra, open the door and let me in."

"Are they out there?" Myra's frail whimper became loud with fear, filled with sudden realization. "Oh, God, honey, get outta the house! Get out before they get you! Go get help!"

As Myra shouted, Groucho ran growling through the open bedroom door at the end of the hall. Naomi turned around and got out of the cat's way, pressing her back to the bathroom door.

She had never heard Groucho growl before. He was a beefy, heavy cat and he made a muted thundering sound on the floor as he sped by. He nearly wiped out in the hall as he made a sudden turn into the kitchen.

Myra began to cry in the bathroom.

Still standing against the door, Naomi slowly turned her head to the right, back to the open bedroom door at the end of the hall. She realized she was holding her breath, and she let it out in a gust of relief when she saw no one in the doorway. She was not sure what she had expected, but seeing Groucho run away growling had given her a shot of adrenaline. The doorway was empty. Naomi turned around and faced the bathroom door again.

"Myra, what's wrong?" she said. "You don't sound good. Please unlock the door and let me—"

"*No*! They'll come in here, they'll come in!"

"Who will?"

Myra cried too hard to respond. She sobbed for a while, then Naomi heard the familiar clatter of Myra's dentures moving around in her mouth. It was immediately followed by another clatter—it sounded as if the dentures had fallen out of her mouth and landed in the sink, clattering against the porcelain.

"Pleathe get help!" Myra said. "Go get help before they get you, pleathe, honey!"

"They? I don't understand who you're—"

A tiny fraction of movement in Naomi's peripheral vision caught her attention. Something at the end of the hall. She jerked her head sharply to the left but saw nothing there at first; just as before, the bedroom doorway appeared empty. But the movement occurred again and tugged her gaze downward.

She thought, at first, that a glove had been dropped on the floor in the doorway, but it moved. Only slightly, a little to one side, but it moved nonetheless. It was not a glove, it was a *spider*, which instantly put her on the verge of screaming with all her might, because she hated and feared spiders, and this one was so damned big that it sent a jolt of panic through her that made her whole body jerk. But a moment later, she saw that what she had thought were the spider's legs were too broad and flat. It was not a spider at all.

Squinting her eyes, Naomi slowly craned her head forward, tried to get a better look without moving from where she stood. An instant before it shot down the hall directly toward her, Naomi realized it was one of the burgundy flowers.

Using its petals as legs, the flower scurried down the hall. The only sound it made was the faint snapping of the sharp thorns at the tip of each petal snagging on the carpet. Somehow, it was the sound as much as anything else that made Naomi scream as she turned and ran.

In the bathroom, Myra shouted, "Go! Get out! Get help!"

Naomi almost ran past the kitchen, but remembered her car keys were on the counter. She threw herself through the doorway at the last instant and her shoulder slammed hard into the corner of the refrigerator. The unexpected impact sent her into a spin and she fell to the floor. Imagining that thing behind her, at her feet, ready to crawl up her leg, she was on her feet in one quick, if clumsy, movement.

Sweeping her keys off the counter as she went by, Naomi stopped at the range and took a heavy black skillet off one of the gas burners on the range. She hefted the skillet in her right hand, then raised it as she turned to face the doorway.

It was not there. The soft snapping sound on the carpet had stopped.

Naomi's arm trembled as she stood with the skillet, poised to strike. Myra had stopped shouting. The only sound was the pouring rain outside. The skillet was heavy and she lowered her arm, turning to find a lighter, more efficient weapon.

Hanging above the counter and below a bank of cupboards were a rolling pin, a few large knives, a meat tenderizer, and a meat cleaver. Naomi imagined one of the things crawling up her leg, and saw herself striking it with the meat cleaver. She was liable to lop off a limb. She settled for the mallet-like meat tenderizer. She put the skillet back on the burner, then reached for the tenderizer, but froze when she heard *ticka-ticka-ticka-tick*.

Snatching the tenderizer off its hook, she spun around, raised it defensively as her eyes grew large. Panic pressed on her chest and she took a deep breath against it, filled her lungs and held it a moment. She let it out slowly through puffed cheeks.

Ticka-ticka-ticka-tick.

That was the sound it made against the old linoleum floor. It was in the kitchen with her. She followed the sound with her eyes and saw the flower hiding beneath the three-inch lip of the cupboards under the counter on the opposite wall.

Her heart throbbed against the back of her tongue. She told herself to calm down. *It's only a—*

"Flower. It's just a flower." The whispered words seemed extraordinarily loud and startled her back into silence.

Flowers don't crawl around, she thought.

She did not take her eyes from it. Neither of them moved.

2

From the park, Lucas had sneaked across three back yards to get to his own. All the back lawns on their side of the street sloped downward to an embankment that looked out over the Granite River's flood plain. That embankment was not visible from most back windows, so he stayed close to it, hid behind fences whenever possible, until he got to his own yard. His black leather shoes were covered with mud and his suit was soaked. He walked along the fence to the side gate, reached over and unlatched it, then opened it slowly, silently.

He had noticed the flowers growing everywhere, but only peripherally, and only because the old man had brought one into the diner and the waitress and the cop had talked about them a bit. Otherwise, he was so preoccupied, he might not have noticed them at all.

Walking over the grass behind the garage, he slowed down as he neared the house. The rain was little more than a drizzle now and not nearly as loud as it had been on his way over. He heard a sound, something familiar. He went to the window of the laundry room, which was always left cracked open a couple of inches. He could see through the laundry room and into the kitchen, where Nancy was pacing, naked and crying, both hands over her face.

Had he chosen their tearful farewell to come sneaking around and spying on them? How long had it been going on? Who was it? The questions raged and swirled in his head like demons trapped in a church.

Still crying, Nancy suddenly disappeared down the hall.

People had cautioned him about marrying so young. They had told him to take time to sow his wild oats. He had not felt the need to plant any grains, wild or otherwise. Of course that did not mean Nancy had no wild oats of her own to unload. Maybe it had taken her eighteen years to realize that, or maybe she had been sowing for a while and he was noticing only now.

Nancy's scream jolted him like an electrical shock. He was about to move from the laundry room window to a kitchen window with a view of the hall when he saw Nancy return to the kitchen holding a broom in one hand. She was still naked and sobbed as she continued to pace.

Shocked into a momentary paralysis, Lucas had absolutely no idea what to do.

3

Carrie watched two men in expensive suits—one fat and carrying a briefcase, the other slender and wearing glasses—get out of a BMW parked at the curb across the street. They came into the diner and she smiled and greeted them with the coffeepot in her right hand and two menus in her left. She led them to a table.

"Do you mind putting us all the way in the back, honey?" the fat man said.

Bristling at the "honey"—she did not mind terms of endearment from regulars she knew, but she did not appreciate them from total strangers—Carrie led them to a booth against the back wall, where they could discuss their important business out of earshot of the yokels, and handed them menus. They turned their mugs upright and she poured coffee for each of them. Both men were somewhere in their forties, Carrie guessed. The thin one had a long forehead and his sand-colored hair was combed over on top in a failed attempt to cover his baldness. The fat man had a full head of short, dark-brown hair shot with some gray streaks and wore black-rimmed glasses. Carrie smiled and said she would be back for their order in a minute, then turned away. She stopped by the sisters' table and freshened their coffee.

The man at the other window table had finished his breakfast quickly. He got up, paid his bill, and left. Carrie found a generous tip on the table as she bussed it.

Vera Pinkston walked in, leaned her umbrella against the wall, and hung her raincoat on the rack. She sat a few seats down from Pete at the counter, near the register.

"I see you got one of those flowers that are everywhere all of a sudden," Vera said as Carrie finished cleaning the table and went behind the counter.

31

"Pete brought that to me," Carrie said as she turned over the mug in front of Vera, dropped a tea bag into it, and poured in some hot water.

Vera came in two or three times a week. A small, stocky woman in her sixties, she lived for yard sales, flea markets, and gambling at Granite River Bingo & Casino while her retired husband built model airplanes. She was an animated talker and wore rings on all of her fingers, so her hands made a lot of clicking noises.

"Find any good yard sales today?" Carrie said.

"In this weather?" Vera said with a wave to the window. "A couple garage sales that were actually *in* the garage, but nothing juicy. I'm just having the tea, Carrie. I'm going to be eating later at the casino."

"They have good food at the restaurant over there?" Pete said.

Vera turned to him with enthusiasm. "Oh, you'd be amazed. They have a buffet. Every day's different. Mexican food, Italian food, Chinese food, all so good, you wouldn't believe it. Eight ninety-nine in the afternoon, ten ninety-nine in the evening. You can eat till you puke."

"Do people gamble more when they're stuffed?" Carrie said.

"Wouldn't be a bit surprised if they did."

Carrie grabbed her order pad from its spot beside the register and returned to the two suits in back. The fat one had papers spread over the table. She smiled as she took their orders.

"Maybe I'll go over there and try it someday," Pete said. "But I'm not a gambling man."

Vera laughed. "Go with me sometime, Pete. I'll fix that."

"You ever win?"

"I won six hundred dollars just last night."

"Did you hang onto it and stop gambling?"

"Oh, don't be silly. I gambled it all away, of course."

"You know, they play subliminal messages in the music they pipe into those places. Messages telling you to lose...lose...lose."

"I haven't heard a thing."

"That's 'cause they're subliminal." Lowering his voice to a mutter, he said, "You should see what they put in the kids' cartoons."

Carrie returned to the counter and frowned at the stem in the small ceramic pot by the register, just inches from Vera's elbow. The flower was gone.

4

"Naomi?" Myra shouted down the hall in the bathroom. "Honey? You okay out there?"

Naomi cleared her throat before responding. "Yeah. Okay."

The flower bobbed up and down on the tips of its petals like a lizard sunning itself on a fence. It moved out from under the lip of the cupboards a few inches—*ticka-ticka-tick*—then backward. Forward again, then backward. It seemed...indecisive.

It had no eyes, but Naomi could not shake the feeling that it was watching her just as closely as she was watching it.

The flower moved toward her again, stopped, then moved a few more inches. Naomi stepped forward, bent her knees, and raised the tenderizer a little higher, ready to bring it down hard. The flower became a blur as it darted to her left—*tickatickatickaticka*—and disappeared through the doorway into the hall. It moved so fast, she was not sure which direction it had gone outside the kitchen, right or left.

Paralyzed by fear and uncertain what to do next, Naomi thought frantically—there were five of them somewhere in the house. Were they *all* moving around? Were they dangerous?

"What the hell is going on?" Naomi muttered as she stood up straight.

At the rear of the kitchen, French doors opened onto a flower garden that Myra had tended as long as Naomi had known her. In recent years, as the insults of age slowed her down, the garden had become more and more overrun with weeds. Now, a small jungle grew outside the doors.

Naomi considered going out the French doors and through the garden to the front yard and her car. But there were even more of the flowers outside. And where would she go for help? What would she say?

Myra Henderson is trapped in her bathroom by crawling flowers! She would get a big laugh. Anyone she told would want to smell her breath. And she knew she could not leave Myra behind.

"They're just flowers," she whispered to herself again. She wondered if Myra had managed to damage any of them before shutting herself up in the bathroom, if all five were healthy and creeping through the house.

Lips pressed tightly together, Naomi breathed through her nose as she willed herself to move forward a step at a time, across the kitchen to the doorway. She tipped her head out into the hall and looked first to the left, then the right.

It was gone. She immediately wondered if it had been there at all. She had seen *something*, but was it an ambulatory flower? Maybe it was just a big spider.

We don't have spiders that big around here, she thought, and it was true. She considered the possibility that it was an exotic pet that had gotten loose. But Naomi knew she was kidding herself.

She clearly had seen the burgundy flower with reflected light shimmering on its black, beaded center scurry across the floor.

With the tenderizer still clutched in her right fist, car keys in her left, she went back down the hall to the bathroom. Making an effort to keep her voice steady, she said, "Unlock the door, Myra, and we'll get out of here, okay?"

"I'm…afraid."

"There's nothing to be afraid of, I promise. It's a…I think it's just a big spider, that's all."

"It'th *not* a thpider," Myra said. She had not put her dentures back in her mouth yet. "I thaw 'em. I watched 'em drop right off their thtems and crawl away."

"*Please* unlock the door, Myra." Naomi winced at the impatience in her voice. She smiled to soften her voice and said, "So we can go, okay? Come on, let's get out of here."

The lock clicked and Myra pulled the door open a couple of inches. She put her toothless face to the opening and peered out with wide, fearful eyes. She whispered, "Are they gone?"

"Well, uh—" Naomi took another look up and down the hall. "—I don't see them. Come on, let's go."

"Lemme get m'teeth. I got tho thcared, I thpit 'em out."

A moment later, Myra pulled the door open. Sliding her dentures into her mouth, she leaned out and looked cautiously up and down the hall.

"I only saw one," Naomi said, "but it ran away. I think maybe they're scared of us. Let's go." She took the old woman's elbow and steered her down the hall to the front of the house. She noticed the big fluffy green slippers on Myra's feet. "You should put on some shoes. It's awfully wet outside."

Myra stopped at the broad archway and peered into the living room. Naomi followed her gaze to a pair of blue-and-white tennis shoes on the floor in front of a rocking chair.

"I'll get them," Naomi said. She put her keys in her pocket as she moved quickly across the living room, hooked a finger in the heel of each shoe, and picked them up. She turned around just in time to see the flower-thing advancing on Myra from behind.

Chapter Three

1

Denise Robillard called Fanny Wheaton at the Green Mist Nursery and asked if anyone had brought in any strange flowers that morning.

"Are you kidding?" Fanny said with a laugh. "I've been swamped. So many people have come in with them, but I've been too busy to take a good look at one yet."

"Have any of your flowers fallen off?"

"What do you mean?"

"The flowers, have any of them fallen off the stem?"

"I don't think so, but I really couldn't tell you at the moment. Have yours fallen off?"

"Either that or someone took them," Denise said.

"I wouldn't be surprised. They're lovely flowers."

"But why not take the whole thing?"

"I'm sorry...what?"

"Do me a favor," Denise said. "When you get a chance to sit down and take a good look at one of them, will you give me a call? I'd like to look over it with you on the phone and see what you have to say about it, because I'm stumped. I've never seen anything remotely like it before."

"Sure, Denise, I'll ring you up."

As she replaced the phone on its base, Denise decided someone had come by while she was in her office and swiped the flowers right off their stems. That had to be it. They were beautiful flowers, after all, and someone had thought enough of them to break them off and take them. That was all.

She kept hearing a sound—*ticka-ticka-ticka-tick*—that seemed to be in the office with her, but she could not find its source. It was irritating, but she had no time to look for it. She had orders to fill.

Denise turned her chair to the monitor and gasped when she saw the flower on her keyboard. It was on her face before she realized it had jumped, and a heartbeat later, Denise was dead.

2

Naomi broke into a run, but she was not fast enough. The flower hopped from the floor to the bottom of Myra's house dress and crawled up the back of it.

Myra screamed and fell against the edge of the archway. "It's on me, it's on me!"

Naomi swung the tenderizer and connected the first time. A thick black goo spattered from beneath the tenderizer when it struck. The flower dropped from Myra's back and landed legs-up on the floor. Naomi stepped back and looked down at it. Most of its legs still twitched, but it appeared too weak to turn itself over. More of the thick black liquid oozed out from under it over the carpet.

"Did I hurt you, Myra?"

"No, no." She turned around slowly. "Is it off?"

Naomi got on one knee and lifted the tenderizer to finish the job, but instead, she bent down for a closer look.

On the black underside of the flower, a sphincter flexed convulsively and, with each spasm, a long, thin, fang-like needle, subtly curved to a vicious point, shot out of it and spurted more of the black goo through its hollow center.

Naomi pounded the flower three more times, then prodded it with the tenderizer and flipped it over. Its beaded center was gone, and only torn threads of the iridescent membrane that had been stretched over it remained attached at the round edges. The petals suddenly looked withered and bruised. The rich burgundy had quickly become a flat, dark brown.

She heard a rustling sound and turned to find Myra sliding down the edge of the archway until she was sitting on the floor with her legs out, dress hiked up. Both hands clutched at her chest and she looked terribly pale. Perspiration glistened above her upper lip and on her forehead.

"Oh, God, is it your heart, Myra?"

A faint nod.

"Where are your pills? Are they with your pills in the kitchen?"

Myra closed her eyes and whimpered as she turned her head from side to side.

"Your bedroom? On the nightstand?"

With another faint nod, Myra wheezed a single word: "Blue."

Naomi ran down the hall to the bedroom. The lamp and telephone took up much of the space on the nightstand just inside the bedroom door. She had to go around the bed to the stand on the other side. On it stood a lamp and fifteen or twenty pill bottles. Some were tall brown vitamin bottles, others were orange prescription bottles. There was only one blue bottle, and

Naomi snatched it up and shook out a couple of pills in her palm on her way back to Myra.

"How many?" Naomi said.

Myra had fallen on her side and formed an L on the floor. Her eyes and mouth were open, but she was not moving.

"Myra!" Naomi knelt in front of her. "Myra, I have your pills."

As soon as she got a closer look at Myra's eyes, Naomi knew she was dead. She hurried to the phone on a small table beside Myra's favorite rocking chair. She picked up the receiver to call 911 but heard no dial tone. It was a land line, and the line was dead.

She hurried into the kitchen and tried the wall phone. It had no dial tone, either.

"Dammit," Naomi said when she realized she had left her cell phone in the car.

Surely the storm was not bad enough to have taken out the phones. Naomi did not have time to think about it. She went back to the living room and quickly stretched Myra out, rolled her onto her back, opened her mouth, and cleared her airway. She began to perform CPR.

3

Officer Perry Milner savored the last few bites of his bacon-and-egg sandwich and listened to Rush Limbaugh. He was parked in his favorite spot, just inside the entrance to the park. It gave him a good view of his beat on Main Street. People coming in from Iron Falls tended to speed after they got off the freeway, and Perry liked to be there to point out the error of their ways.

He finished the sandwich and stuffed the wrapper into the paper bag. Sipped the coffee, tilted the rearview down, and removed his cap. He frowned at his hair in the mirror as he ran his fingers through it, messed with it. It was the bane of his existence. It was why he wore his cap all the time, even though it was not necessary. His chocolate-colored hair grew in all directions and was completely unmanageable. Suzy joked that he had a whole head of cowlicks.

A friend of a friend had once recommended that Perry see an expensive hairdresser named Froi in Iron Falls. He had made the appointment, shown up, taken a seat in the chair. Froi examined his hair, ran his fingers through it, then a comb, all the while clicking his tongue and shaking his head, sometimes rolling his eyes. Finally, he said, "Your hair grows in too many directions at once. I will be having nightmares about your hair when I am ninety years old and can't remember what I had for lunch. I'm sorry, but I refuse to deal with this." Froi wished him luck and sent him on his way. After that, Perry went to Lewis Freekirk, his usual barber in Mount Crag, once a week, kept his hair cut pretty short, and hoped for the best. He put his cap back on and readjusted the mirror.

Rush Limbaugh broke for a commercial and Perry lit up a Marlboro, took his cell phone from the glove box, and called home. Suzy sounded miserably congested.

"I just wanted to see how you were feeling," he said.

"Awful. I'm still in bed. I haven't done anything this morning."

"What's so important that it has to be done this morning? Stay in bed."

"I'll have to get up when the kids come home from school, though."

"Why? They can take care of themselves. They're just gonna stare at their screens, anyway."

"The house is a mess, and I'll have to cook dinner."

"Would you stop it? I'll bring home pizzas. The kids'll love it. I'll make you chicken soup when I get home, okay? I love you."

She laughed, but it turned into a cough. "I love you, too."

He turned off the cell phone and finished his coffee. He dropped the empty cup into the bag. A couple of yards from the car stood a garbage can with a concrete base and a metal top. He wadded up the bag, got out of the car, and hurried through the rain to the can, tossed the bag in, and started to go back to his cruiser. But he stopped when something on the ground caught his eye.

It was a flower identical to the one Pete had brought Carrie in the diner. But this flower was not on a stem. It lay atop the mottled carpet of dead leaves on the grass. It was pretty, and Perry thought Suzy might appreciate it. He could put it in a bowl of water beside the bed.

Perry bent down to pick up the flower, and it crawled a few inches toward him.

He stood up straight and said, "What the *fuck*." He frowned at it for a moment, waited for it to move again. It remained still on the leaves. He decided he had not seen it move after all. The rain was disturbing the leaves on the grass. That was probably what had caused the flower to appear to move.

He bent down again to pick it up.

The flower blurred as it crawled up his arm and latched onto the upper half of his face, knocking the cap off his head. Perry was dead before he hit the ground.

4

"Pete, what happened to my flower?" Carrie said.

"Whassat?" He cupped a hand to his right ear and turned it to her, then spotted the bare stem. "Hey, what happened to your flower?"

"I don't know."

Vera said, "You know, a minute ago, I thought I heard a little sound behind me while I was talking to Pete, but I didn't pay any attention to it."

"But where *is* it?" Carrie said. She searched the floor in front of the counter. When she found nothing, she went behind the counter and looked around again.

At the order window, she said, "Gustav, did you see what happened to this flower on the counter out here?"

"Flower?" he growled. "What I got time for flower for? I don't know nothing 'bout no flower."

Carrie looked around the counter one more time, but it was gone.

"It's got to be around here someplace," Vera said.

"You'd think." Behind the counter, Carrie stood with a hand on her hip, flummoxed.

"Well, it didn't just get up and walk away," Vera said.

"Maybe it wasn't a flower."

Carrie and Vera turned to Pete when he spoke.

"And what else would it be?" Carrie said.

Pete shrugged. "Maybe it's some kind of, I don't know, a…a drone, sort of."

"Government or alien?" Carrie said.

He rolled his eyes and smirked as he turned back to the newspaper.

"You need to start watching TV, Pete," Vera said. "Turn off the damned radio."

From the order window, Gustav said, "Short stack, eggs over medium."

Carrie took the breakfasts to the two suits in the back booth. The fat one gathered up all the papers he had spread over the table and slipped them back into his briefcase beside him on the bench. The men did not stop talking or even glance at her as she set down their plates. She knew the type. She did not expect much of a tip, if any.

"Enjoy your breakfast," she said, even though she knew they were deaf to anything she had to say.

Returning to the counter, she half expected to see the flower in some place she had missed, or right out in the open, in plain sight. When it did not happen, she folded her arms across her chest and sighed.

"Don't worry," Vera said with a playfully dismissive wave, her beringed fingers rattling together. "It'll turn up."

"'Maybe it's a drone' is crazy but 'It'll turn up' makes sense?" Pete said. "You think it stepped outside for a smoke?"
"That's enough, you two," Carrie said with a chuckle that sounded hollow and nervous.

5

Lucas stood outside looking into the small window over the kitchen sink. It was open a crack. He was beginning to wonder if he had been wrong.

Still naked, Nancy was moving around the house in tears with a broom, occasionally crying out. She went in and out of the kitchen looking as if she were not quite sure where she was going or what she was doing.

She had not been in the kitchen for a few minutes, but he could still hear her crying somewhere else in the house—the living room, maybe. He had expected to find her with a lover, but it seemed she was alone in the house. Had his suspicions and gut feelings all been the product of his imagination?

Perhaps he had not lost those old insecurities after all. But he could not understand what was wrong with Nancy.

Suddenly, she came into the kitchen again and cried out.

"Get away from me!" she shouted as she attacked something on the floor with the broom. Then she stepped back and her eyes seemed to follow something as it moved over the floor and out of the kitchen. When she looked up, she turned, and her eyes fell on Lucas.

He considered ducking, but it was already too late. She had seen him.

Nancy blinked several times and stepped toward the window. "Lucas?" she said.

Lucas stepped away from the window and went to the back door. Nancy unlocked it and let him in. He tracked mud on the floor, but she did not notice.

Her hair was a mess and her tears had created smudges of mascara around her eyes. As they clutched the broom like a rifle, her hands trembled. "What are you doing here?" she said. "Why aren't you at work?"

I took the day off so I could come here and catch you in the act of having an affair, he thought, but he said nothing.

Nancy dropped the broom and came to him, embraced him, and sobbed against his shoulder. She held him so tightly, it made his back hurt. Between sobs, she said, "He's dead. He's dead."

"Who's dead?"

"Steve. I'm sorry, Lucas. I'm so sorry. I didn't mean to hurt you, I don't know how it happened. Please don't hate me. Please don't—"

"You're having an affair."

She became silent and a moment later, nodded against his shoulder.

"That's why I came," Lucas said. "I suspected as much. I wanted to catch you. I figured he'd be here with you."

"He is. Was." She started sobbing again. "He's in the bedroom. He's dead."

6

Crying and out of breath, Naomi gave up. She was unable to revive Myra. Feeling suddenly exhausted, she slowly stood, then dropped onto the couch and buried her face in her hands.

Somewhere in the house, Groucho meowed.

Naomi slowly lifted her face from her hands. Her attention had been focused on Myra. She had forgotten for a while about the flowers—four of them now, as far as she knew—crawling around the house.

She looked all around the living room, but the only flower she could see lay broken on its back in the hall just outside the archway. She got up and looked for the meat tenderizer but could not remember where she had dropped it. After about a minute, she decided to get another weapon instead.

With a glance down the hall, she saw no flowers. She did not see Groucho, either, but heard him meow again and followed the sound to the kitchen.

Sweeping her eyes over the kitchen floor before she entered, Naomi found Groucho sitting on the windowsill, and as soon as he saw her, his meows increased in frequency and became distressed and insistent.

"Hey, Groucho," she said, her voice high and breathy as she looked all around the kitchen. "You're gonna be okay." She went to the counter and took the meat cleaver off its hook. Before she turned around, Groucho hopped up on the counter and she yelped and jumped with surprise. "You scared the shit out of me, cat," she said as she stroked his back. He purred and rubbed against her.

Naomi decided she had to get out of there—out of the kitchen and out of the house. She went down the hall to the front door, pulled it open, and took in a sharp breath.

Two of the flowers were clinging to the outside of the screen door. There was another on the porch steps, two more on the walkway, a few on the grass, and one on the hood of her forest-green SUV.

They're everywhere, she thought. *How many times did I hear those words today?*

She closed the door.

Groucho meowed pleadingly in the kitchen.

Naomi turned around and headed for the open door of Myra's bedroom at the end of the hall. It was not a very long hallway, but now it seemed to stretch on forever. She knew if the other two phones in the house were dead, there was no reason to believe the phone in the bedroom would work, but she had to try it. If not, she would have to brave the many flowers waiting outside.

When she passed the kitchen doorway, Groucho came out into the hall and followed her the rest of the way to the bedroom.

Standing just outside the doorway, Naomi reached in with her left hand and flipped on the light. It was a cluttered room. There were stacks of quilts everywhere. Myra used to make them before her arthritis became too severe.

The phone was on the stand beside Myra's bed next to the lamp. It was straight ahead, just a few feet away, no more than two steps. She took them.

Groucho stayed outside the bedroom in the hall.

Naomi reached for the receiver as a flower skittered up from between the nightstand and bed to her hand.

Chapter Four

1

Mr. Pittfield, the owner of the small Save-King chain, had not shown up yet, so Chuck took the time to go back to the florist counter to see if Denise had identified the strange flowers yet. He found the flat Mrs. Tucker had brought in still on the counter, but the stems were naked. All three flowers were gone. Frowning, Chuck went around the counter and peered into Denise's office.

She was stretched out in her chair at her keyboard, arms hanging limp at her sides, legs splayed. From where he stood, he could not see her face. She appeared to be asleep. But Denise was a hard worker who would never sleep on the job, and Chuck knew with a chill that something was wrong.

"Denise?" he said as he went to the doorway of the office.

From somewhere in the small room, Chuck heard a quiet slurping sound. Denise's head was hanging over the edge of the chair's back, mouth open, and one of the burgundy flowers was on her forehead.

Confused, Chuck frowned. He said her name again, quieter than before, and a little distracted, because his attention was on the flower, which was moving quickly and with rhythm. With each movement, it made a quiet, wet, slurping sound. He cocked his head to one side as he realized the flower was thrusting aggressively on Denise's forehead.

Blood on Denise's cheek, a tiny crimson gem slowly trickling down and leaving a trail, had come from the thorn at the tip of one of the flower's petals, which was buried deep in her flesh.

Its petals tense, thorns dug in for leverage, the flower rapidly humped Denise's forehead. But it was slowing down now.

"Jesus Christ!" Chuck said after staring for a few seconds to take it all in. "Denise!"

He stepped into the office and tried to pull the flower off, but its hold on Denise's head was strong and firm. Chuck was astonished by the flower's strength. It felt muscular in his grip, resisting his pull as its movements became slower, gradually weaker.

As he struggled to pull it off of Denise, he saw that the flower had changed. The center with the iridescent sheen was no longer plump and beaded. It was now flat, and the shimmering membrane that covered it was wrinkled and deflated.

The flower stopped moving. Suddenly, it peeled off Denise's head without resistance. Chuck dropped it to the floor and stepped back with alarm.

The flower flipped through the air and landed with its thorny petals pointing up. Chuck saw the needle-like appendage sticking out of the center. It glinted with moisture. But he did not have time to look any closer.

He put his fingertips to Denise's throat but could not find a pulse. He lifted an eyelid with his thumb. Her eye stared blindly, dull and flat. She was dead.

There was something wet in her hair and he bent forward to get a closer look. It was blood. A small hole had been made in Denise's skull just above her hairline.

He grabbed the receiver off the wall phone just outside the office, but before he punched in 911, he spotted Toby Noonan walking by. He shouted, "Toby! Come here." Chuck keyed 911.

Toby was nineteen, blond and muscular, a lifeguard in the summer months and a favorite of many of the store's female customers. He turned and came to Chuck's side.

Chuck nodded his head to the office doorway. "Something's wrong with Denise. You know CPR, don't you?"

"Yeah."

"Get in there."

Toby rounded the counter and went into the office.

2

Naomi screamed as she flung her hand upward and catapulted the unprepared flower into the air. It made an arc through the bedroom doorway, over Groucho, and landed on the floor in the hall. Groucho turned around, faced it, and hissed, ears flattening as his back arched.

The adrenaline rush made Naomi's hands shake, but she kept her eyes on the flower, suddenly drenched with perspiration and out of breath. Groucho hissed again and slinked backward.

"Come on, Groucho," she said. "Come on in here. Kitty-kitty." She forced herself to take a step forward. Then another. "Kitty-kitty. Come on, Groucho." She held the meat cleaver ready as she stood in the doorway. The flower in the kitchen had seemed afraid of her—maybe she could scare this one.

It did not move from its spot on the right side of the hall, three feet in front of Groucho. It did not move at all. It was nothing more than a lovely flower plucked from its stem, lying on the floor.

"Groucho, come on. Come in here."

But the cat did not move, either. He was no longer backing off. Instead, he positioned himself to pounce, head low, ass in the air.

"No, Groucho, don't do that." Naomi bent down to pick him up, but she was too slow.

As Groucho bounded forward with a deep, chesty growl, the flower reared up on four petals.

Naomi cried out.

It hopped onto Groucho's face and closed its petals around the cat's head. Groucho flopped onto his back and kicked his hind legs frantically with a garbled yowl, trying to dislodge the creature. When that did not work, the cat got to his feet again and zigzagged blindly down the hall, hitting the walls a few times. The flower did not let go, kept its petals tightly closed on Groucho's face and head. The cat disappeared into the living room.

The yowling stopped abruptly. Naomi listened for movement, but did not hear a sound. Making her way down the hall was like walking in waist-deep water. She stopped, listened again, and heard a faint, wet sound. A distant slurping. She passed the kitchen and moved to the far right side of the hallway, against the wall, moving away from the archway even as she neared it.

She saw Myra's feet first, then the bookcase. It contained the complete set of Nancy Drew mysteries Myra had bought for her daughters when they were little girls, as well as books by Ruth

Rendell, Lillian Jackson Braun, and other mystery writers. Another step and she saw the end of the couch below the rectangular front window that looked out on the yard and driveway, and Myra's legs. She kept her eyes on the floor, searching.

Naomi stopped a moment and turned around. There was nothing on the floor behind her. Not at the moment, anyway.

"Okay," she whispered to herself as she turned toward the living room again, "No more screwing around."

Jaw set, she took the next few steps quickly and decisively, and went into the living room, cleaver held outward and level with her shoulder. But she winced as she stepped over Myra.

A wind had come up and blew rain against the window. There had been a fire in the fireplace the first time Naomi had come in that morning, but all that remained now were embers. It took her a moment to find Groucho. He was stretched out on the floor at the other end of the couch, near the fireplace hearth.

"Oh, Groucho," she said in a high, sad voice as she put a hand to her mouth. She took a few steps more and stopped. His tongue was stretched out on the cream carpet. The poor cat looked as if he had died while in the middle of a convulsion, all four legs stretched outward—front legs pointing forward, back legs pointing backward—tail straight, mouth open, and eyes wide.

The flower was lying on the floor a couple of inches in front of Groucho's face. It looked like a spider on its back. She watched it for several seconds, but it did not move. It appeared smaller now, withered and browned.

Naomi went to the end of the sofa, sat on the rolled arm and bent forward between her knees to get a better look. The fang-like needle, ever so slightly curved, was fully extended in the center of the flower.

"It's not a flower," she whispered.

It might have been on the end of a stem that appeared to have grown out of the ground, but it was no flower. Flowers did not pop off their stems and crawl around. Flowers did not cut phone lines, and Naomi had a feeling in her gut that those creatures were responsible for the dead phones.

"Flowers don't kill cats," she whispered.

There was a hole in the center of Groucho's head. A trickle of blood had stopped between his eyes, vivid on the white fur of his forehead.

Naomi stood and entered the kitchen from the living room, through the small dining area, and went back to the knives hanging on hooks beneath the cupboard over the counter. She looked them over and chose a butcher knife with a black handle and a shiny, broad eight-inch blade.

Naomi was determined to get to her SUV, and to her cell phone, which was in her purse on the passenger seat. She checked to make sure her keys were in her pocket. They were.

She wondered how many other people were having problems similar to hers. The flowers were everywhere; people had been saying those words all over the place, all day, *They're everywhere!* Surely she was not the only one now being terrorized by them. She thought of the three flowers in the flat Mrs. Tucker had left with Denise at the Save-King and worried about Chuck—and Denise, who was likely to be closest to the flowers.

Naomi turned to leave the kitchen and found Groucho standing in the doorway to the hall, watching her. She stared at the cat with her mouth open for several seconds, then said, "Groucho?"

Without making a sound, the cat jumped on her. The shock of Groucho's claws digging into her skin made Naomi drop both her weapons and scream as she fell backward and hit the floor.

3

"I'm hungry now," Vera Pinkston said to no one in particular at the counter in the diner.

"You want something?" Carrie said. She was distracted by the fact that she had been unable to find the missing flower. Her eyes kept returning to the bare stem.

"I had a banana before I left the house this morning, I figured that would hold me till I get to the casino buffet to stuff my face around noon or one, but dammit, I was wrong. Give me a Swiss cheese omelet and extra crispy hash browns. No toast."

Carrie wrote out the order, turned around, clamped the ticket onto the carousel in the order window and gave it a spin so it was on Gustav's side. She did not see Gustav in the kitchen. She assumed he had taken advantage of the slow-down to go to the restroom. She took another tour of the tables with both coffee pots, regular and decaf. When she returned to the counter, she poured some regular in Pete's cup.

He shook his head and said, "I've never understood the appeal of yard sales, myself. My wife used to go to 'em and always brought home a bunch of junk. Other people's junk, that's all it is. I mean, if *they* don't want it, why the hell would *I* want it?"

"I saw a woman on *Antiques Roadshow*," Vera said. "She and her husband found a box of comic books at a garage sale. Five bucks. They took it home to their teenage son, who liked to read comic books. Well, he knew a thing or two about comics, and he recognized some very rare editions in the box. They were rare, all right. Long story short, the contents of that box turned out to be worth something like thirty thousand dollars, according to the appraiser on the show."

Pete chuckled. "How often does *that* happen?"

"But you never know," Vera said. "That's the fun. Each yard sale holds the possibility of treasure. It's a new adventure every time."

Pete shook his head. "An adventure in other people's junk."

Carrie laughed as she glanced over her shoulder at the order window and did a double-take.

The ticket for Vera's omelet remained untouched on the carousel. She walked over to the window. "Gustav?"

A sound came from the floor in the kitchen. Carrie stood on her tiptoes and poked her head as far as she could through the order window. It was enough to see a sliver of Gustav's white back. He was lying on the floor.

"Oh, no," she said as she hurried through the swinging door next to the order window. When she entered the kitchen, Gustav was on hands and knees, getting to his feet with his back to Carrie. "Gustav, are you all right? What happened? Are you hurt?"

He stood up straight, a hulking figure with legs like tree trunks. He wore his long white apron over a white T-shirt and dark-green pants. He did not move for a long moment.

"Gustav? Are you all right?" Carrie took another step toward him. "Can you hear me?"

He turned around slowly.

Carrie gasped when she saw the hole in his bald head. "Gustav, what *happened*?" She stepped toward him and reached out to touch his shoulder, but he punched her in the face with a beefy fist. Carrie dropped unconscious to the floor.

"Hey!" Pete shouted.

"I saw that!" Vera said as she pounded a fist on the countertop.

Gustav ignored them and walked past the order window and out of their line of sight.

Vera got off her chair.

55

"Wait," Pete said with concern. He turned his chair to face her, looked at the window again, then back at Vera. "I don't know if you should go in there. He's a big guy and…well, he might've just snapped. You know, he might be…nuts."

"I want to see if Carrie's all right." Vera went behind the counter to the swinging door.

By the time she got to the kitchen, Gustav was gone.

4

Toby Noonan managed to get Denise on the floor, flat on her back, and began to administer CPR. His hands were shaking because she was dead. He had never dealt with a dead person before. Nor with a living person. So far, Toby had only performed CPR on the dummy they used in the classes.

He was rhythmically pressing on Denise's sternum when she punched him in the jaw and knocked him on his back. The room darkened for a moment, and bright-white specks floated around against a field of gray in front of his eyes. Before he could recover, Denise straddled his hips and pressed her hands flat on his chest, holding him down on the tile floor.

She looked down at him with a slack, dead face as she placed a hand beneath his chin and pressed his head back hard against the floor.

Toby gawked up at her, stunned. He felt something tentatively touch top of his head. After a moment of hesitation, it crawled up the crown of his skull to his forehead. He began to struggle and said, "Hey, hey, wait a minute, what the hell are you—"

There was a moment of bright, searing pain, then nothing at all.

5

Lucas stared down at the dead man lying naked on his bed and struggled with the storm of emotions that raged through him. On the pillow beside the man's head lay a shriveled, dead flower.

He had never seen the man before. It was a relief that Nancy had not been carrying on with one of his friends. His name was Steve Dreyfuss, she had told him, and he had come from the computer store to work on the kids' computer when it was on the fritz a few months ago. Steve certainly did not look like a computer geek. He was in his late twenties, maybe ten years younger than Nancy, and had pretty-boy looks, soft, almost feminine features, a strong jaw, blond hair in a buzz-cut. He was the kind of guy who, in his teens, probably looked like he belonged in a boy band. He was exactly the kind of guy Lucas would expect to see someone like Nancy with—the beautiful cheerleader and the popular pretty-boy. They were perfect for each other. Steve was younger, better looking, in better shape, and even more generously endowed than Lucas. He sighed and shook his head and muttered, "This has turned out to be a pretty shitty day. And it's not even noon yet."

His eyes kept returning to the small hole in the top of Steve's forehead. It was plainly visible through his short, blond hair. There was a spattering of blood around it. It was tiny, from a small-caliber weapon. But not too tiny to kill him.

They had no guns in the house, and Lucas wondered where Nancy had gotten the weapon. He looked around the bedroom for it. On the nightstand stood a vase that held a number of long, green, thorny stems. Bare stems with no flowers on them. He stepped over to the vase and frowned down at the naked stems. Was it some kind of in-joke between them, something only they found funny? Lucas realized that the possibility that private little jokes had grown between them was even more painful than the fact that they had been having sex in their bed.

57

He turned to the bedroom door, but was not sure he was ready to go back downstairs to the kitchen and face Nancy again. She had killed a man. And she had been babbling something about flowers, something that made no sense.

Was she having some kind of breakdown? Why had she killed the man? Had he tried to break it off? Had she been in love with him?

Suddenly, Lucas felt like vomiting. But he gulped a few times, resisted the urge to gag, and it passed. He took a few deep breaths, then left the bedroom and went slowly down the stairs. He was stunned. It could not be enough that Nancy was guilty of the infidelity he had suspected, no, that would not have been a big enough blow by itself. It needed something extra, something to give it a kick. How about...*murder*!

He wondered if he could have prevented it had he arrived a little earlier, then tried to imagine a situation in which Nancy would kill someone. Could it have been self-defense? Had Stevie, the pretty-boy computer nerd, tried to hurt her? The questions were endless, but he knew they made no difference. A man was dead. He would have to call the police.

6

The fall knocked the breath from Naomi's lungs.

With its claws hooked into her shoulders and ribs, the cat bit the edge of her jaw on the right side of her face. She closed both hands on the animal and tore it off of her. The pain was like fire as the claws ripped out of her flesh. She threw it as hard as she could across the kitchen. The cat tumbled through the air and hit the floor on its side as Naomi scrambled to her hands and knees and looked for the knife and meat cleaver.

The cat was back on all fours again almost instantly.

She spotted the cleaver a few feet away beneath one of the chairs at the Formica table.

Naomi and the cat started moving at the same time, she on hands and knees for the cleaver, the cat for her. She swung the cleaver just in time to hit the cat with its broad, flat side, striking even harder than intended and knocking Groucho up in the air and into the sink.

Getting quickly to her feet, she hurried across the kitchen, through the doorway, and down the hall, cleaver in one hand, car keys in the other. Her skin burned where the cat's claws had been torn out and an intense stinging persisted in her jaw where she had been bitten.

Sounds from the kitchen. Claws clicketing against the floor, pawing for traction.

She had seen the hole in Groucho's head, his tongue hanging out. He was *dead*. But it did not seem to be slowing him down now. That creature had done something to him. That was why Groucho did not make a sound while attacking her. Somehow, it was no longer Groucho.

The hall stretched out before her, the front door so far away at the other end. The pain was excruciating. She felt the warm trickling of blood leaking from the wounds beneath her clothes.

Claws pierced the skin on her back and she screamed in pain as she stumbled to a stop. She turned and slammed her back against the wall. The claws deepened their hold. As she reached both hands back over her shoulder and clutched for the animal's head, Naomi made a sound that surprised her—she growled. The cat bit her left thumb and she cried out.

Staggering down the hall a bit, she slammed her back against the wall again, near the kitchen doorway. She rolled back and forth, pressing the cat hard between her back and the wall, heels dug into the carpet as she pushed backward. The instant she felt the claws retract, she stood up straight and the cat dropped off her back. She started running before she realized which direction she was headed. Burning with pain, front and back, she lost her footing for a moment, then fell through the kitchen doorway, landed on her side, and slid over the floor a few feet.

It was under the table in the dining room several feet away, a single flower-creature beneath one of the four matching chairs at the small but handsome oak dining table. It kept its petals low and hugged the carpet, as if to avoid being seen.

The clickety sound of claws on the floor. Groucho's claws.

She had been distracted by the creature under the chair and was not prepared. The cat was on her again. She tried to sit up, but when it bit her neck, she dropped back down again. Putting the cleaver on the floor, she closed both hands hard on the cat's body, tore its claws out of her back and shoulders, and threw it across the kitchen once again.

She glanced to her left and screamed. The flower-creature was now two feet from her face, petals bent sharply, ready to spring. She grabbed the cleaver and rolled toward the thing, raised the cleaver to strike it. The creature quickly retreated to its spot under the chair beneath the dining table.

"Jesus Christ!" she said aloud, thinking, *The cat* wants *me on the floor!*

Claws on the floor again, getting close.

Naomi sat up and swung the cleaver as if she were swinging backhand with her tennis racket. The flat side of the blade made hard contact with the side of the cat once again, knocked it against a cupboard, dropping it to the floor. In that moment, as the cat lay on its right side, Naomi got to her knees, raised the cleaver, and brought the blade down across the cat's abdomen and spine.

She felt bone break beneath the blade and the cat's forelegs began to twitch. A sob-like sound escaped her as she lifted the cleaver and brought it down again. This time, she lopped off the cat's head. The broken body became still as the head rolled to the right.

The eyes looked at her and narrowed. The mouth spat. The tongue moved.

Naomi screamed.

She swung the cleaver again and the blade opened the cat's head in a splash of thick, warm, black fluid, viscous and heavy. It spattered the cupboard and Naomi's hands and arms and face.

The head, split almost completely into two pieces, made no more sounds.

Struggling to her feet, she turned toward the dining area, the black-smeared cleaver held ready. She listened for its thorns snagging on the carpet in the dining room, but heard nothing. She searched the carpet, but did not find it.

They were working together, she thought. *The cat kept me on the floor while the flower-thing…but why? So that thing could poke a hole in* my *head the way it did Myra's? So it could—oh, God, so it could use me the way it used Groucho.*

She went to the sink, put down the cleaver, and quickly washed her hands of the black goo. As she washed her face, she reminded herself there were still three more of those creatures crawling around the house.

She dried her hands and face on a yellow hand towel hanging from a hoop on the side of the cupboard, then turned around and leaned her hips against the edge of the sink. She was bleeding, her wounds were on fire, and she was winded and perspiring. Her hands trembled and adrenaline was still raging through her, making her heart pound. She felt ready to come out of her skin, but she intended to get out the front door and to her SUV, to her cell phone. But she stood there a while and gave herself a moment to calm down.

7

"What's going on out there?" Pete said. He turned at the counter and looked out the window onto Main Street. It was the second scream they had heard outside in the last fifteen or twenty seconds.

Carrie had heard it, too, and she went to the door and peered through the glass. She saw someone running down the sidewalk across the street. "Is that Sybil Brubaker?"

"She came high-tailing out of Shirley's salon a few seconds ago," Mrs. Fridley said. "I think she was the one who screamed."

Mrs. Sturgis nodded. "She was, I saw her."

Across the street, Sybil Brubaker, a heavyset woman of fifty-two with a swirl of blonde hair on her head, ran as she probably had not run in many years to her Lincoln parked at the curb, got in, and started the engine. The car lurched away from the curb, and she sped down the street. Once she was gone, though, Carrie saw no one else on the street, on foot or driving a car. She opened the door and stepped out onto the sidewalk.

The rain had stopped. It was so quiet and still, she heard the muted click of the traffic light change from red to green at the intersection up the block, with no one there to take advantage of it. It was a stillness that made her uneasy. She turned and went back inside the diner.

"Here," Vera said as she handed Carrie a bag of ice cubes wrapped in a small towel. "Your eye is almost swollen shut, honey. Put that on it for a while."

In the full-length mirror on the wall by the coat rack, Carrie saw that her left cheek and eye were swollen and turning various shades of purple. All she remembered was Gustav's enormous fist swallowing up the whole world, and then she was on the floor with Vera hovering over her. By the time she had pulled herself together and gone to find Gustav, he was long gone. She had looked out the back door and had found that his white pickup truck was no longer in the small parking lot behind the diner. *Hasta la vista, baby,* as Gustav, a big fan of Arnold Schwarzenegger, was sometimes inclined to say. She had gone back inside and taken a couple of aspirin for her headache.

Placing the small bundle of ice against the side of her face, Carrie returned to the kitchen, and Vera followed.

"What are you looking for, hon?" Vera said.

Carrie bent down to get a better look at the shriveled lump on the floor. She nudged it with the toe of her sneaker. It was the flower, but it looked as if it had quickly wilted and died.

"What's that doing in here?" Vera said.

"Good question."

"Doesn't hold up well off the stem, does it?"

Through the order window, Carrie heard Mrs. Fridley say, "That wind is sure blowing those strange flowers all over the place out there."

Carrie went back out front to the door. The bundle of ice covered her eye as well as her cheek, so she could see only with her right eye.

Footsteps approached behind her and Pete said over her shoulder, "Wind?"

She saw one of the flowers skitter across the street. It was followed a moment later by another.

"Wind's not blowing out there," Pete said, quietly but firmly.

The firmness in his voice could not conceal his nervousness, and Carrie was afraid. The flowers—or whatever they were—used their petals to zip over the pavement like spiders. They became wine-colored blurs as they—there went another one!

She went to the phone by the register. Placing the ice on the deck behind the counter, she picked up the phone receiver and called the Green Mist Nursery. If anyone in town knew anything about the flowers it would be Fanny Wheaton or her husband Donald.

Mrs. Fridley and Mrs. Sturgis were looking out the window. Mrs. Sturgis said, "No, that's not the wind. Are you sure those are flowers?"

"It almost looks like they're crawling around, doesn't it?" Mrs. Fridley said.

Mrs. Sturgis clicked her tongue and shook her head. "They *are* crawling around, you ninny. Didn't you see that last one? It was *crawling*. On the *ground*."

While she waited for an answer, Carrie looked around at her customers. The two men in suits had finished their breakfast, but she had not taken their plates or given them their bill yet. They had been talking to each other quietly the whole time and had paid no attention to anyone or anything else. They probably had not even noticed Gustav punching her lights out. The fat man had gotten some of his papers out again, and they were handing them back and forth. Now he gathered them up again and put them back in his briefcase, then they stood. The fat man looked over at her and smiled.

"Could we have our check, please, honey?" he said.

"Sure thing." She realized she had been waiting on the phone a long time without an answer and handed the receiver to Vera, who was back in her seat at the counter, and said, "I'm trying to call the nursery. When someone answers, ask if they know anything about the flowers."

"Okay." Vera put the receiver to her ear and rested her elbow on the countertop.

Carrie met the two suits at the register and wrote up their bill. "Look, I don't think it's a good idea to go out there right now," she said as the fat man offered her a Visa card.

"Why's that?" he said.

The slender man said, "Looks like it stopped raining."

Carrie shook her head. "No, I mean, there are things crawling around out there. Something…strange is going on."

"Well, we have to be somewhere," the fat man said just before belching softly.

She took the card and the men started talking to each other as if she had gone away. Something about quarterly reports. She wondered what had brought them to Mount Crag. When she finished ringing up their bill, she said, "I'm serious, guys. There's something out there."

"She's right," Mrs. Sturgis said. "I just saw another one."

But the fat man simply smiled at her and said, "Thank you," as they turned away, and she knew he had not heard a word she had said.

The men went on talking as they put on their overcoats, then went out the door.

"There's no answer," Vera said as she handed the receiver back to Carrie.

She frowned as she put it to her ear. "Why would there be no answer at the nursery?" she muttered.

Because something's wrong, she thought as she placed the receiver back in its cradle. Her throat felt constricted as she thought again, *Something's wrong.*

Carrie looked out the window and saw the two suits walk across Main Street to the BMW parked at the curb in front of the hardware store, still talking the entire way. As the fat man opened the door on the driver's side, one of the flowers crawled up to his heels and stopped.

"Uh-oh," Mrs. Fridley said.

Carrie stepped out from behind the counter and moved closer to the window to get a better look.

As the fat man pulled the door all the way open, the flower scurried up the back of his leg and disappeared beneath his overcoat. He dropped his keys and did a wiggling dance, turning in a small circle, waving his arms.

"Oh, God!" Mrs. Sturgis said, turning away. She did not want to watch.

Carrie held her breath as the man struggled.

And then it was on his face. He screamed once—a high, shrill sound that made Carrie shudder even though it was muffled by distance in the diner—then dropped to the ground in a limp heap. The other man had gone down already on the other side of the car.

Everyone in the diner gasped. Pete got up and came to Carrie's side.

"Looks like I was wrong and they aren't drones after all," he said, voiced lowered almost to a whisper.

"Very funny, Pete."

"I'm not gloating. I *was* wrong. They're not drones. They're...*creatures*. Which do you think sounds crazier? Drone flowers or flower creatures?"

"I'm really not in the mood, Pete."

"No, *no*. Think about it. If they were drone flowers, you'd think it was a government thing, right? But flower *creatures*? Where would something like *that* come from?"

"I don't know," Carrie said, "but we're not letting any in *here*." She looked around and said, "No one leaves for a while, okay? And nobody comes in."

Vera said, "I don't think anybody *wants* to go out there."

Carrie went back to the phone and called the police. Pete followed her and talked in a low voice as she waited for an answer.

"Look, I was listening to Larry Baker on the radio this morning and callers were talking about those flowers and how the ground was burnt where they grew up, and how some people saw bright lights—like 'falling stars' one caller said—shoot out of the clouds and fall to the ground last night. Whassat sound like to you?"

"You're saying you think these things are from outer space?"

"I hope you're not saying that's a crazy theory at this point, because if so, you need to do the math. Meteor shower, little thingies fall to the ground, strange flowers grow up out of black spots of burnt earth, flowers pop off stems and, I don't know, they fuck people up, is what it looks like to me, you want the truth. You got a better equation than that? 'Cause if you do, I'm wide open."

Carrie did not have a better equation, but she had a growing stomachache. She looked out the window as Perry Milner drove by in his cruiser and her chin dropped in shock. There was a man lying in the street, and Perry sped by as if he were not there.

Carrie thought, *Something's* very *wrong.* She put the receiver on the counter and, for a moment, ignored her call to the police. She fished her cell phone from her pocket and called home. Her mother answered.

"Mom, I want you to lock up the house and stay inside until I get home."

"What on *earth* are you talking about, Carrie?"

"Have you been outside this morning?"

"Just to feed the dog. Why?"

"Have you seen the flowers?"

"Those strange flowers that have popped up everywhere? Yes, I've seen them. Where in the world did they come from?"

"You've got to stay away from those flowers, Mom. They're, uh…they're toxic. They're causing real problems here in town. Just lock up the house and stay inside until I get home, okay? And don't let anyone in. I'll call you again as soon as I can, okay?"

As she slipped her phone back into her pocket, Carrie wondered if Robby was safe at school. She picked up the receiver. Still ringing. It probably would be best, she decided, to close up the diner as soon as she could, go get Robby, and take him home. Whatever was happening, she wanted to be home with her family when it happened.

Chapter Five

1

Chuck moved quickly through the store, eyes scanning the floor for the other two flowers. He glanced at the hands of people he passed to see if they had picked up one or both. He found neither of them.

He had not finished preparing for Mr. Pittfield's arrival, but that no longer mattered. Chuck worried about Denise, and the possibility that others in the store could be harmed. He considered an evacuation, but decided to wait. He went back to the florist counter to check on Toby before going out front to meet the paramedics.

Toby was gone, and so was Denise. Another of the flowers lay on the floor looking desiccated. That left one flower somewhere in the store.

"What the hell," he said as he left the office and the florist counter. Had the ambulance already come and gone? He spotted Tina Rainer walking by. She was one of the baggers, a skinny teenager with braces. "Tina, did the ambulance already leave?"

"What ambulance?"

"Have you seen Denise or Toby?"

"Yeah, just a minute ago," she said. "They went out there." She pointed to the nearest bank of four automatic glass doors, two entrances and two exits.

"They went outside?"

"Yeah. Toby's head was bleeding."

"His head. You mean, his forehead?"

"Yeah."

"They just *walked* out of the store?"

"Yeah."

"How long ago?"

She shrugged. "I don't know. A couple minutes, maybe?"

Denise had no pulse, he thought. *She was dead.*

Chuck rushed to the doors, went outside, and scanned the parking lot, the sidewalks, even the street. If Denise and Toby had come outside, they were already gone. Where would they go? He turned and went back in the store.

He thought of the two withered and bruised-looking flowers on the floor of Denise's office. One for Denise, one for Toby—and now they were both gone, Denise after dying with a hole in her head, and Toby bleeding from the forehead. He thought of the long, sharp appendage sticking out of the bottom of the flower that had fallen off Denise, and again of the small hole in her head.

Those flowers did something to them, he thought.

Another thought hit Chuck with the force of a blow to the solar plexus. Naomi had said Myra Henderson had five of those flowers in her house. And Naomi had been on her way over there.

He rushed back to the florist counter, grabbed the receiver from the phone on the wall, and hit two buttons to connect him to the office upstairs. His assistant manager, Mike Newman, was on a break, and he always spent his breaks in the office. Mike answered.

Chuck said, "Get on the PA and evacuate the store right now."

"What? Evacuate—*what*?"

"Just do it. I have to go out. Do it now. Get everyone out of the store. I don't have time to explain."

"But Pittfield is coming and we—"

"Tell him I'll explain when I get back."

"Are you *kidding*? He'll have a stroke."

"Can't be helped. Do it, Mike. Get everybody out. *Everybody*. I want this store empty when I come back." He put the receiver back on its hook and broke into a run.

He left the store, ran across the parking lot to the far end where employees parked, and got into his pickup truck. His Marlin lever-action .44 Magnum rifle was on its rack across the back window, and he had ammo in the glove box. He reached beneath the seat to make sure his .45 Colt Commander was there, along with a spare magazine. In Granite County, any law-abiding citizen who filed for one could get a permit to carry a concealed weapon, and Chuck had one. Since she had met him, so did Naomi.

As he pulled out of the parking lot, he took his cell phone from the seat, and flipped it open. Naomi was such a frequent visitor of hers that Chuck had Myra's number in his cell phone. The sound of the phone trilling at the other end of the line went on and on. Chuck became alarmed—he knew Myra had an answering machine that should pick up, but it did not. He closed the phone, put it down, and pressed his foot on the gas pedal.

2

Lucas took the phone from its base on the kitchen counter.

Nancy stepped over to him. "What are you doing?"

"I'm calling the police."

"Do you think they'll believe us?"

He could not get a dial tone on the phone. "Did you cut the phone line, or something?"

"Did I *what*?"

He put the phone back on the counter. "What have you done, Nancy?" he whispered.

She frowned above her raccoon smear of mascara. "What are you talking about?"

He closed his hands on her upper arms and shook her gently. "Why did you kill him?"

Her eyes widened.

Lucas said, "Where's the gun? Where did you get it?"

"Gun?"

"Where *is* it?"

She jerked from his hold and took a couple of steps backward. "Lucas, I've been trying to *tell* you, I didn't kill him. One of the flowers did it."

"One of the flowers." He sighed.

"He brought me a bouquet of those strange flowers that bloomed everywhere this morning. I put them in a vase, then put it on the stand next to the bed. We were…when we…they fell off. All the flowers, they just fell off their stems and crawled away."

"They *crawled* away? Nancy. Are you *hearing* yourself? I mean, do you really expect me to believe—"

"One of them got on his head. There was…nothing I could do. It held on so tightly. It was so strong." She stopped to look all around her feet, turned completely around scanning the floor. "I'm not sure how many there are, but they're running loose in the house."

72

"Who's running loose in the house?"

"The flowers. And there are probably more outside. They're everywhere."

"Nancy, look at me."

She faced him and he looked into her eyes. He wondered if she had been doing any drugs, but there was nothing wrong with her eyes besides being puffy and wet from crying.

"Will you take me out of here, Lucas?" she whispered. "Please? I'll put some clothes on and we can go, okay? We can go someplace safe."

He watched her tremble and felt like crying. What had happened to her? He thought back over the last few months. Had her behavior been that of a married woman hiding an affair? Or had it been the behavior of a woman struggling with mental illness?

"What really happened, Nancy?" he said. "Tell me the truth, please. Why did you kill him?"

"Goddammit, I did not kill him! And if we don't get out of here, those flowers will do the same thing to us that they did to him. It just happened, Lucas, a few minutes before I saw you at the window. It happened right in *front* of me. There was nothing I could do."

"Is that what you're going to tell the police? That a flower killed him?"

"That's what I *mean*, they're not going to *believe* us! Oh, Jesus, Lucas, please, let's get *out* of here."

He searched his pockets for his cell phone, then remembered he had left it in the car. He turned and went to the back door. "I'll be back in a couple minutes," he said. "I'm going to get the car."

"You're *leaving* me here? With *them*? But they're all over the house! You can't just—"

"I'll be right back." He went out the door and closed it behind him. He made the walk back to his car quickly, got in, and drove out of the park to his house. He parked in the driveway next to their white Toyota Sienna. He took his cell phone from the passenger seat, opened it, and punched in 911. As he waited for an answer, he walked into the house, went down the hall to the kitchen, and gasped.

Nancy was lying on the floor on her back, arms spread, ankles crossed. The broom lay a couple of feet away from her on the floor. A withered flower clung to her hair.

Lucas closed the cell phone and slapped it onto the counter, then knelt beside Nancy. He knocked the dead flower off her head. There was blood in her hair and he cradled her head in his arm.

"Nancy? Nancy, answer—oh, Jesus," he said when he saw the small hole. He touched her throat, but felt no pulse. Wrapping his arms around her, he held her still body close.

3

Naomi left the kitchen in a hurry. She walked quickly down the hall to the front door and opened it. The creatures that had been clinging to the screen door were gone, but there were still others on the ground outside. She ran her tongue back and forth along her lower lip as she plotted her route to the SUV. *Step on them whenever possible*, she thought, *smash them like bugs*. But she knew they jumped, so she would have to move fast. Once she opened the screen door, she could not afford to hesitate for a second.

She held the cleaver in her right hand and put her left on the handle of the screen door. Her heart felt like it was trying to punch its way through her rib cage. She took a deep breath.

Jerked backward by her hair, she lost her footing and screamed as she was dragged away from the door and thrown to the floor in the living room. Her torn and bleeding back hurt when it hit the floor and she grunted. Her scalp felt electrified.

Myra stood over her, but she knew it was not really Myra. Naomi had no doubts that Myra was dead. This person, this creature, did not move like Myra, and it said nothing—she would be talking her head off by now.

The large old woman stepped over, then straddled her. She sat on Naomi's thighs, pressed her hands to Naomi's shoulders, and pinned her to the floor.

She kicked and flailed her arms, but Myra weighed a *lot*. She struck the old woman with the meat cleaver. The blade became wedged in Myra's left side, between two of her ribs, but Naomi did not let go of the handle. As she tried to pull it out, she glanced to her right.

Moving slowly and cautiously, one of the flower-creatures crawled through the archway from the dining room and into the living room. It came directly toward her.

Naomi screamed.

The meat cleaver budged, but would not come free of Myra's ribs.

She could hear the snicketing of the creature's thorns on the carpet, snagging those little threads and snapping them, growing louder in her right ear as it drew closer to her head.

4

Chuck parked his pickup beside Naomi's SUV, got out, and took the Colt from beneath the seat. He racked the slide, then tucked it under his pants above his right thigh. He put the extra magazine in his left back pocket, took the Marlin from its rack, got a box of bullets from the glove box, and loaded the rifle. He put a couple of handfuls of ammo into the right front pocket of his pants.

On his way through town, Chuck had seen a man lying on the side of the street with a flower on his face. Three times, he had seen flowers dart across the street and disappear under parked cars. He had tried without success to run over each one. Oddest of all was the lack of traffic; his was the only vehicle on Main Street, and he saw no pedestrians out in the rain. There were usually a few, even in a town as small as Mount Crag. Even in bad weather someone was always going somewhere, but the town appeared abandoned.

Chuck was on the front walk when he heard Naomi scream. Flowers skittered over the ground away from him as he ran to the front door, which stood open with the screen closed. He opened it, went inside, kicked the door closed as he went into the living room, and quickly took in the situation.

Shouldering the rifle, he trained it on the flower moving slowly toward Naomi. It suddenly rushed forward and Chuck fired. The explosion of black goo spattered over Naomi's face and Myra's leg and hip.

5

Lucas felt a surge of panic when he realized that Nancy's killer—and, he now knew, Steve's killer as well—could still be in the house with him. Looking down at Nancy through his tears, he lowered her gently to the floor and stood. He turned to find Steve standing just inside the doorway, still naked but very much alive.

He was taller than Lucas, too.

Lucas said, "Uh...I thought you were, uh..."

Steve took a few steps toward him and punched him hard in the face. Lucas went down beside Nancy and Steve was on him before he could recover from the punch, straddling him and holding him down.

Lucas heard a clicking sound on the tile floor nearby and turned his head. A beautiful burgundy flower lay on the floor a couple of feet from his face.

His nose was bleeding and his head ached.

The flower crawled toward him.

"Oh, Jesus," Lucas said, thinking, *She was telling the truth.*

He started to struggle as the flower climbed up over his face, and it occurred to him, once again, what a shitty day it had been.

Lucas Rowland died with a lot of unanswered questions on his mind.

6

The meat cleaver finally jerked free of Myra's ribs. Naomi held onto it even though her hand was cramping.

"Get her off of me, Chuck," Naomi said with panic loud in her voice. "It's not Myra. Myra died."

Chuck lifted his right foot, put it on Myra's shoulder, and shoved her off of Naomi, who scrambled to her feet at Chuck's side.

"What the hell is going on?" he said, voice low and quavering.

"It's those damned flowers. They're not flowers."

Myra got to her feet, face expressionless and slack.

"Shoot her in the head," Naomi said. "It's not Myra, Chuck. Myra died of a heart attack earlier. It's whatever that flower injected into her skull. That's where you've got to shoot her, Chuck."

"Same thing happened to Denise and Toby," he said. He put the rifle in his left hand and used his grab to take the .45 tucked into his pants. He aimed as Myra started toward them and fired.

The bullet made a small hole just above her left eyebrow, and below the one left by the flower creature. But it made a larger one as it exited the back of her skull in a splash of thick black goo and chunky brain matter. Myra's body dropped to its knees, then fell forward. On the floor, the body convulsed violently for a few seconds before falling still.

"Oh, my God," Naomi said. She turned to Chuck and clung to him as he put an arm around her. She felt very close to falling to pieces, to collapsing into a sobbing, wailing heap on the floor where she stood. It had been bad enough to see Myra die once that day, but a second time was almost more than she could bear. The moment passed, and she held herself together. She pulled away from him, took a deep breath, turned away from the body on the floor, then looked all around the living room. "There are two more of those things left in here, somewhere."

"Then let's get out of here before they catch up with us."

"Wait. I've *got* to get this stuff off my face. Come with me to the kitchen."

In the kitchen, she washed her face and hands, then dried them thoroughly.

"Here," Chuck said as he handed Naomi the rifle. "You know how to use this." He took the rounds from his pocket, gave them to her, and she put them in the pocket of her jeans.

She had a Marlin of her own at home. While she did not go hunting with Chuck, she had taken a gun safety course, and they did a lot of target- and skeet-shooting together. Naomi had thought she would hate shooting a gun until Chuck had talked her into trying it. It had been so much fun she had begun regularly visiting the shooting range in Iron Falls by herself when he had to work. Since falling for Chuck, guns had become a hobby. When most of her friends got an urge to go shopping, they bought clothes, shoes, and cosmetics; Naomi bought a new gun.

She cradled the Marlin in her right arm with ease and held the meat cleaver in her left hand. They left the kitchen and went down the hall. Chuck opened the front door and they looked out through the screen.

"There's a lot of them out there," he said, "but they ran away from me as I was coming up to the door."

Naomi nodded. "They seem to be afraid of us. Unless they have someone our size who's helping them out."

"You can explain that to me in the truck. Let's run all the way there and wave our arms around and make some noise."

Naomi took a deep breath and blew it out hard. "Okay. Let's go."

Chuck kicked the screen door open and they ran out of the house shouting like lunatics.

7

Officer Perry Milner parked his cruiser in the lot behind the Mount Crag Police Station and entered the back door with his service revolver drawn. To his immediate right was the glass-enclosed dispatch office. Janine Cooley was in there, standing by the coffeepot on the counter, pouring herself a cup. Perry opened the door, stepped inside, and she glanced over her shoulder.

"Hey, Perry," she said, then put her head down again, attention back on her coffee. "What can I do for you?"

He said nothing.

Janine poured sweetener into her coffee. The spoon chimed against the sides of her mug as she stirred. She picked up the mug, took the spoon from it, and turned around.

Perry raised the gun.

Janine's mouth fell open and she dropped the spoon. Perry fired at the same instant the spoon hit the floor. The bullet entered just below Janine's right eye and she dropped to the floor with the spoon.

Perry spun around and stood in the doorway of the dispatch room, his gun aimed at the door directly across the hall. It was Chief Ledbetter's office, and the chief could be heard cursing inside. A few seconds passed and the door opened. Chief Ledbetter said, "What in the hell is going on out—" Perry fired and shot him in the chest. The chief fell backward into his office and lay with his feet sticking out of the doorway into the hall. Perry quickly went into the office and dropped to one knee beside him. He removed from Ledbetter's belt a ring of keys. The chief stirred and groaned, and Perry put the gun to Ledbetter's forehead and fired. He stood and put the keys in his pocket.

In the dispatch room, a phone trilled once, twice.

Perry hurried down the hall and around the corner, footsteps silent on the carpet, and around a corner to the left, to the combination reception and records area at the front of the building. Renee Crofts was already on the phone at the front desk, calling for help. He put a bullet into the side of her head. She dropped forward and her head thunked hard on the desk. Blood cascaded from her nose and pooled over papers and folders. Perry reached over the counter and hung up the phone.

The pleasant trilling in the dispatch room continued.

The door that opened onto the small front lobby was always kept locked. If someone in the lobby needed to get into the back, Renee or someone else had to let them in. Perry unlocked the door, then opened it and crossed the lobby's tile floor to the glass door and opened it. Damp, chilly air wafted in.

A concrete walk led up to the police station door, which was set back in an alcove in the front of the red-brick building. The flagpole stood in the center of a rectangle of green grass. Hedges grew along the perimeter of the front parking lot. As Perry stepped out the door, very little of the rectangle of grass was visible. Instead of green, the lawn was the color of red wine. The grass was covered with flowers. None of them moved, not one. They looked as if they had been carefully spread out over the ground.

A few people stood waiting for Perry in the alcove, and as he held the door open, they stepped into the station. Denise Robillard and Toby Noonan went in first, followed by Donald and Fanny Wheaton, then Gustav. No one spoke. Once they were inside, Perry remained standing at the door, holding it open. A section of the lovely burgundy smear on the ground broke away and funneled into the open door. Perry saw more people headed toward the station, including a naked man and woman. He followed the flowers, about twenty of them, back into the station and let the door gently swing closed.

A cacophonous clattering rose from the lobby's floor as the thorns rattled over the tiles. They followed Perry into the back, where the snagging sounds the flowers made on the carpet sounded like popcorn being popped in another room.

The phone in the dispatch room continued to trill.

Perry went in back to the break room and removed the chief's keys from his pocket. Denise, Toby, Donald, Fanny, and Gustav followed him. They did not speak, though their eyes occasionally met.

It was the largest room in the station and doubled for breaks and briefings. A large rectangular table stood in the center with chairs around it. Near the table were two vending machines, one with snacks, another with sodas. In an alcove to one side were the doors to the restrooms. The chief was an amateur photographer, and some of his photographs of Mount Crag and the surrounding area were framed and on the walls.

The phone in the dispatch room fell silent.

A toilet flushed in the men's room. They turned to the restroom door.

Several seconds later, the door opened and Officer Gary Bennis stepped out and saw Perry, saying, "I could've sworn I heard—" He looked around at the others and frowned. Then he looked down at the flowers all over the floor.

Gustav stood nearest Bennis and he brought the officer down with a single blow of his enormous fist. He got down beside the cop and put a knee on his chest. One of the flowers quickly mounted his forehead. Bennis cried out, but he was abruptly silenced and became still. Gustav stood as the flower began to noisily pump its contents into Bennis's skull.

Perry turned to the door of the weapons room. He had to try a few of the keys on the chief's ring before he found the right one. Reaching into the small room to turn on the light, he looked at all the guns on their racks. Then he stepped into the room and started handing out firearms to the others.

8

When Carrie got no answer at the police station after almost five minutes of waiting, she hung up the phone. If no one answered there, something was definitely wrong.

"He's up!" Mrs. Sturgis said.

Carrie came out from behind the counter and returned to the window. She stood next to the table where Mrs. Fridley and Mrs. Sturgis sat. There were autumn leaves and acorns painted in the corners of the pane, but Carrie had a clear view of the two men.

The slender suit on the other side of the BMW was on his feet. He stood there not moving, staring at nothing in particular, for what seemed a long time. Carrie saw the tiny dark spot on his head and what looked like a dribble of blood. It was very small from where she stood, and she might not have noticed it if it were not for the fact that she had seen the same thing at the top of Gustav's forehead before being knocked unconscious.

The fat man got to his feet. He did not stir and get up slowly like a man who just regained consciousness, but instead got directly to his feet and stood straighter than he had before he was attacked.

The two men walked away from the car and stood in the middle of Main Street looking at each other. Flowers emerged from beneath parked cars along the street and Carrie's mouth slowly opened in shock as they pooled together around the men's feet and then stopped moving. As if waiting.

"Oh, God, what *are* those things?" Mrs. Sturgis said in a hissy whisper.

"I think we can all agree," Carrie said, somewhat distressed by the tremble she heard in her own voice, "that they're not flowers."

A great laugh bellowed from Pete, who stood at the door looking through the glass.

The two suits stood there looking at each other for nearly a full minute. When they finally moved, they turned and looked directly through the window at Carrie.

She took in a sharp breath and stepped away from the glass.

The flowers parted and made a path as the men walked toward the diner. They moved with some stiffness that seemed to loosen up with movement. And they moved with purpose.

Carrie hurried around the empty table at the window and threw herself at the door and locked the deadbolt. Unfortunately, within the wooden frame, most of the door was a rectangular pane of glass. She looked through the glass and saw the men heading straight for the door. Turning and rushing over to the register on jets of adrenaline, she opened a drawer beneath it and removed a Browning 9mm pistol. It had been her dad's. He had taught her how to use it and had bought her one to keep at home as well. She still went to the shooting range in Iron Falls once every few months to keep from getting rusty.

She realized that Vera and Pete and Mrs. Fridley and Mrs. Sturgis were watching her closely. She turned to Vera and said, "Get on the phone and call 911. I called the police station, but didn't get an answer. If you get an answer, tell them to send help right away."

Vera said, "What if I don't?"

"Then I guess we're on our own."

Vera left her seat, rounded the counter, and went to the phone by the register.

Carrie moved in front of the counter and faced the door, where Pete stood with his back to her.

"There's no dial tone," Vera said. "It's dead."

"What's going on?" Mrs. Fridley said. There was a quaver of fear in her voice. Mrs. Sturgis reached over and took her hand.

"I may have been wrong about this, Carrie," Pete said.

"What?"

"About this being an invasion."

"Oh, for crying out *loud*, Pete—"

"This looks more like some kind of test run."

"—*stop* with that stuff, will you?"

The fat man reached the door first and found it locked. He looked through the glass at Carrie. She saw a trickle of blood that had dribbled from his hairline onto his forehead. Just like the other guy, and just like Gustav.

And just like how many other people in town right now? Carrie wondered.

The slender man stood behind the fat man, and behind them both on the sidewalk were the flowers—forty, maybe fifty of them—all stirring, moving in place, as if impatient to surge forward. Carrie looked down at them and felt momentarily dizzy. Flowers were not supposed to move around like that, and watching them gave her the disorienting sensation of being in a dream and being awake at the same time.

The fat man rattled the door hard. He placed both hands flat against the glass. His face was slack and expressionless as he looked in at Carrie, eyes dull and staring.

"Step aside, Pete," she said, and he did. She raised the gun and racked the slide to let him know she meant business.

He just stood there for a long moment, looking in. Behind him, the slender man looked over his shoulder. Then the fat man turned around.

Carrie took a step back and leaned against the edge of the counter by the register. Relief began to move through her now that the man had turned away and appeared to be leaving.

But he did not leave. Instead, he jabbed his elbow backward into the glass. Carrie gasped. The first time failed, but the second blow broke the glass with a loud clatter. Large shards of it fell away, leaving long fangs of glass in the wooden frame.

Mrs. Fridley screamed.

Still behind the counter, Vera said, "Oh, shit."

A single laugh barked from Pete and he said, "Oh, yeah, this is some kind of fuckin' *test run*," and then he laughed again as he looked around at everyone. "Sure as hell looks that way to *me*, anyway."

The fat man turned around, reached his arm through the opening, and groped for the deadbolt.

"Stay out or I'll shoot!" Carrie shouted.

He turned the lock, pulled his arm back out, turned the knob and pushed the door open.

Mrs. Fridley and Mrs. Sturgis screamed together in a kind of harmonious dissonance.

Carrie aimed at the fat man and fired once, twice.

His large, heavy body quaked with each gunshot. Then he stepped into the diner.

Chapter Six

1

"Something fell out of the sky last night besides the Leonids," Naomi said as Chuck drove the pickup down Yardley Street. "Just like Myra said."

"What do you mean?" Chuck said.

"Both Myra and Mrs. Tucker said the flowers grew up out of little black spots on the ground, as if the ground had been burnt by something. All morning, I've been listening to people on the radio say they saw things falling out of the sky in the direction of Mount Crag."

Chuck shook his head. "Naomi, the Leonids are meteors that—"

"I'm not talking about the Leonids, I'm talking about something *else*. Something that used the Leonid shower as a cover."

He frowned. "You're saying they're from outer space?"

"Well, let's see. They're flowers that aren't really flowers. They pop off their stems and crawl around and jump like spiders. They kill people by injecting black goo into their skulls, and then the dead bodies get up, walk around, and hold other people down while the flowers do the same to them. Yeah, I think outer space makes sense, don't you?"

"As much sense as anything else, I guess."

They had run from the house waving their arms and shouting, and the creatures had scattered on the ground before them. Chuck had gone out of his way to step on several of them. They had smashed underfoot with a soft crunch, and the thick black substance that filled the center of each flower splashed out from under his shoe when he stomped on them, like the guts of a large squashed bug.

As they drove away from Myra's house, Naomi had noticed something that gave her a chill. The brown-and-green stems were still standing everywhere she looked, but the flowers were gone. For each of those stems there was, somewhere, a flower crawling around looking for someone into whom it could deposit its contents.

She picked up Chuck's cell phone on the seat between them and called her mother.

"How are you feeling, Mom?"

"I'm achy today, as usual, but I'll live," Laura said.

"Look, I want you to stay inside, okay?"

"I wasn't planning to go anywhere."

"Good. Just stay inside. Don't even go out on the porch. And make sure all the doors and windows are closed and locked."

Laura laughed. "What? Why?"

"Please, Mom, just do it, okay? I'll explain it all later."

"Is something wrong?"

"Yes, something's wrong, but I don't have time to talk about it now. As long as you stay locked up in the house, though, you'll be fine. Now, hang up and go make sure all the doors and windows are shut and locked, and don't let anyone in. I don't care who it is, Mom, even if it's someone you know. Don't answer the door unless it's me, okay?"

"You're scaring me, Naomi."

"I'm sorry, I don't mean to. Just do everything I said, okay? Please? I love you, and I'll get there as soon as I can." After the call, she turned to Chuck. "You want to call your parents?"

"They're in Iron Falls this morning. They both had doctor appointments."

Naomi turned on the radio and tuned to the news-talk station in Iron Falls. There were no radio stations in Mount Crag. Larry Baker's show was over and calls were being fielded by Wanda King now. After listening for a couple of minutes, Naomi realized they were discussing local politics. There was no mention of trouble in Mount Crag.

"They're not talking about it," she said. "How can they not be talking about it? The callers wouldn't talk about anything else on Larry Baker's show."

Chuck turned off of Yardley onto Main Street. His pickup was the only vehicle on the road. There were no pedestrians on the sidewalks.

"What's this?" Naomi said.

Chuck slowed the pickup as they neared the Pantry Shelf diner. A fat man in a suit had just broken the glass in the diner's door and was reaching in while another man in a suit stood behind him.

Naomi's eyes were drawn down to the movement of a cluster of flowers around the men's feet.

"Oh, shit, Carrie's going to need help," she said.

Chuck pulled over and double-parked next to a minivan across the street and up the block from the diner. He got out and Naomi slid across the seat and exited on his side. They jogged across the street, the .45 in Chuck's right hand while Naomi held the rifle.

89

They reached the sidewalk just as the two men in suits entered the diner. Screaming was followed by gunfire. Chuck stopped, aimed his gun at the flowers just outside the door, and fired. There was a burst of black and the flowers scattered in a flurry of blurred movement.

Naomi shouldered the rifle, got a bead on one of the creatures, and squeezed the trigger. Viscous black liquid spattered as the flower skidded over the sidewalk, then tumbled a few times before coming to a stop with its petal-legs up.

There was another gunshot from inside the diner.

"Carrie!" Naomi called. "Shoot them in the head!" She took a shot at a scurrying flower, but missed. They were skittering away in all directions, hiding under cars, disappearing around corners.

A gun fired again inside, and again.

Chuck approached the diner's entrance and Naomi followed as the thinner of the two men in suits turned to face them in the doorway.

Naomi saw the small hole in his forehead, the dribble of blood.

Chuck raised the Colt and fired. A second hole appeared just above the bridge of his nose and he collapsed into convulsions in the doorway. He became still after several seconds. A few feet beyond him lay the fat man on his back, his right eye now a gunshot wound.

Someone in the diner screamed, and Carrie shouted, "Naomi?"

"I'm out here, Carrie." She stepped over to the open doorway and peered inside without getting too close to the dead man. Carrie stood in front of the register, a gun held at her side. Her left hand was pressed against the side of her head and she wore an expression of pale, open-mouthed horror.

"They're in here," Carrie said. "Those things, those flowers, there's a lot of them in here."

"Step on them," Naomi said. "Like bugs. And don't let them near your head!"

Chuck bent down and grabbed the lapel of the man's suit coat, dragged him out of the doorway, and left him against the wall, just beneath the window. Naomi stepped forward to go into the diner, but stopped when several flowers skittered out. After that, a few more shot over the threshold, and she paused again before going inside. She carefully stepped over the broken glass around the doorway.

Pete bobbed up and down, his knees shooting up as he enthusiastically stomped on the creatures, elbows kicking up at his sides as he laughed, crushing the flowers beneath his worn old boots as if he were dancing at a hoedown. "Gotcha, you sumbitch!"

Mrs. Fridley stood on her chair, while her sister, Mrs. Sturgis, was making an effort to step on the flowers, but they moved too fast for her. Tears glistened on Mrs. Sturgis's cheeks, and she wore an expression of terror and disgust, but she kept going after the creatures on the floor.

Then the sound of their thorns on the tile floor stopped. There were no more of them in the diner. No one moved for a long moment and a heavy silence fell over the restaurant. Carrie broke it when she began to sob.

Naomi went to her and embraced her. "You had to do it, Carrie," she said. "They were going to hold you down and let one of those things...well, they were going to kill you."

Carrie took a deep breath and calmed her sobs. "I thought they were dead. They were lying beside the road after those flowers got to them earlier."

"They were dead," Naomi said.

"But how could they—"

"We don't know how yet," Chuck said, "but that's what they're doing. Can everyone here get to your car and go home?"

Mrs. Sturgis took her sister's hand as Mrs. Fridley got down off the chair. "I'm parked just outside," Mrs. Sturgis said.

"I'm parked up the block a ways," Vera said.

"Can I catch a ride with you, Vera?" Pete said. "I walked here from my trailer."

"Sure, Pete, no problem."

"If you have guns at home," Chuck said, "load them. Make sure you don't have any of those flowers inside your house and *keep* them out."

"And don't let anyone in," Naomi said as she pulled away from Carrie but left an arm around her shoulders. "Look for a small hole at the top of the forehead, maybe a little bit of blood. Those flowers poke a hole in the skull and inject something. It kills the victim, but then the…the thing uses the victim's body." She turned her head to Carrie. "The man you shot was already dead, I promise."

"I've got to get my son at school and take him home," Carrie said. "I've got to go pick up Robby."

"Whatever you do," Naomi said to all of them, "don't let those things anywhere near your head. Wave your arms, move fast, and make a lot of noise, and they'll probably stay away from you. Unless they have help, which is why you have to watch for people with a small wound in the forehead. They are *not* your friends."

Mrs. Sturgis went to the register and said, "We should pay our bill and—"

"Pay it next Friday," Carrie said. "You, too, Pete and Vera. Don't worry about it. Everybody be careful and get home safe."

The sisters and Pete and Vera left the diner.

"I've got to go," Carrie said. "I'm parked in the back. I'll see you two later."

"What do you want to do about the front door?" Chuck said.

Carrie put both hands on her hips and stared at the shattered glass in the door. "I'll take the cash drawer with me and worry about the door later."

Naomi and Chuck left the diner when Carrie did. They went back to the pickup across the street.

Chuck started the truck and said, "I hope the store hasn't completely fallen apart since I left."

As he drove away, Naomi said, "I'm starting to think the entire town has fallen apart."

Along Main Street, Naomi saw faces in the windows of shops and restaurants. They were the frightened, worried faces of people who knew something was terribly wrong outside but had no idea what.

They were passing the Safeway when there were, in an instant, people with guns in the street, two of them naked, and they were firing.

The pickup's left front tire blew. A web of cracks appeared in the right side of the windshield.

"Get down!" Chuck shouted.

Naomi ducked below the dashboard as he brought the pickup to a stop.

"Oh, my God," Chuck said.

"What?" When she heard no more gunfire, Naomi slowly sat up and looked out the shattered windshield. "Gustav!"

"And Denise. And Toby."

"Donald and Fanny."

With them were a naked man and woman, and a man in a dark-gray suit. Carrie recognized him as the stranger seated at the counter reading the newspaper in the diner that morning. All of them were armed with shotguns and revolvers, and around their feet, spreading out over the road in a growing pool of burgundy, were more flowers.

Somewhere in the distance, a deep throbbing sound began to grow louder.

2

Carrie drove her almond-colored Volvo to Mount Crag Middle School and parked at the curb directly in front of the entrance, near a sign that read NO PARKING. There were two police cruisers parked in front of the building, both empty. She hoped they were there for security reasons and not because there had been trouble already. She put her purse strap over her right shoulder and left her car. On her way into the building, she checked her watch. It was a few minutes after noon, so she would try the cafeteria first, then she would go to the front office and ask.

The building seemed unusually quiet considering it was the lunch hour. She stopped at a classroom to look inside through the window in the door. It was empty. She moved on to another, and it was empty as well. Down the main corridor, she turned left and went down another hallway. At the end, double doors led outside, to a covered sidewalk that led to the cafeteria.

Something was wrong. There were usually kids wandering the halls at lunchtime, and the cafeteria was always so loud you could hear the kids inside well before you reached the building. She did not hear a sound as she opened the door and stepped into the building.

It was empty.

Alarm sent adrenaline surging through her.

Maybe there's an assembly in the gym, she thought as she hurried out of the cafeteria and ran across the grass. There were no signs of life, no one walking around the small campus, no faces in windows. She went past the back of the main building and over to the gymnasium.

There were two double-door entrances to the gym. One of them had been left ajar. Carrie pulled the door open, stepped inside, and made a small sound of horror into her palm.

A large portion of the shiny hardwood floor was covered with children lying on their backs. The faculty was there, too—Carrie recognized some of Robby's teachers—all stretched out close together on the gymnasium floor. Four police officers walked around the edges of the horizontal crowd with service revolvers drawn.

Two of the officers saw Carrie. She recognized their faces as they hurried toward her; she did not know their names but had seen them around town. They rushed toward her with odd, slack expressions on their faces. On the forehead of one, she saw a smear of blood, but it was too late. The other one got behind her and pressed the barrel of his gun to the back of her head. The other gestured with his gun for her to follow him. He walked a couple of steps ahead of her but kept looking back at her.

"Mom!" Robby called. He rose to his feet in the mass of children lying on the floor. "Over here!"

One of the officers standing on the other side of the gymnasium fired his gun into the air. The sound reverberated in the gymnasium. Robby quickly got back down on the floor.

"Robby, I'm coming," Carrie said. She broke away from her uniformed escorts and hurried toward Robby, carefully stepping over and around the children on the floor. She reached her right hand into her purse and found the Browning 9mm, flipped the safety off. Robby got up on his knees as she approached him. She bent down and hugged him tightly with her left arm, her right hand still in the purse. "Come on, we're getting out of here." She pulled him to his feet.

"But, Mom—"

"Ssshhh." She put her arm around him and led him back through the obstacle course of children.

The officer who had pressed the barrel of his gun to the back of Carrie's head fired into the air.

With her heart beating so fast she feared she might actually have a heart attack, Carrie kept going with Robby. They stepped over the last child and headed for the front door.

The police officer who had just fired his gun into the air stepped in front of her and she stopped. He stood only three feet away when she took the 9mm from her purse, raised it, and fired. She missed the first time, but fired again immediately.

The officer dropped to the floor and convulsed.

Carrie quickly stepped around him and headed for the doors.

There was another gunshot. This time, Carrie felt as if someone kicked her hard in her lower back, so hard that she was knocked to the floor. She did not let go of Robby, and pulled him down with her.

A horrible, burning pain blossomed on her right side and spread all the way across. She rolled onto her left side, pulled her jacket back, and turned to look down at her waist. A dark stain was spreading fast over the right side of her green sweatshirt. The pain spread with it and beyond it, somehow moving through her entire body. It even made her heartbeat feel like a deep drumming that vibrated in her bones as it pounded harder and louder, until she realized it was not her heartbeat but something outside. Something overhead that grew louder as it passed, then began to fade.

3

Naomi and Chuck remained hunkered down in the pickup, their heads close. They heard no more gunfire, but that other sound grew louder and more familiar.

"A helicopter," Naomi said. "Maybe somebody's coming to help." It sounded like a *big* helicopter.

"Well, whoever called them should be given the key to the city and a medal."

"Let's get out," Naomi said.

He nodded, then kissed her on the mouth. He sat up.

Naomi sat up, too, her rifle beside her, the butt on the floorboard, the barrel leaning against the edge of the seat.

They were just standing there. The man in the suit stepped forward. He held a shotgun, gestured with it, beckoning silently for them to come out of the pickup.

The helicopter grew louder fast until it was shaking the entire pickup truck. Its large shadow slid over them ominously as the helicopter passed low and descended into the Safeway parking lot. It was black, shiny, and broad, and it gave Naomi the impression of a giant insect lighting on the pavement.

"I *really* hope they've come to help," Naomi said, choosing to ignore the tremble in her voice.

"If they have, great, but we've got to focus," Chuck said. "You can pick them off at a distance. I'll save my ammo until they're closer."

"Roll down the windows," Naomi whispered, "and we can shoot from behind the doors."

They rolled down their windows, then waited a moment. The man in the suit beckoned with the shotgun again.

"Come out shooting," Chuck said, "and aim high."

Naomi opened her door, got out, and shouldered the rifle with the barrel poking out through the door's open window. She aimed for the forehead of the man in the suit, and fired.

He collapsed and convulsed on the ground for several seconds.

She took aim at the naked man as the others began to fire at the pickup truck. Her next shot was as successful as her first.

Gustav blew out another tire with his shotgun, then charged forward, heading directly for Chuck, who was hiding behind his door, peeking over the bottom edge of the window. The enormous man drew closer, and Chuck raised his gun. He fired, and the bullet tore a slice of skin off Gustav's left temple but did not pierce the skull.

Gustav stumbled backward, but kept his footing. He stood and swayed a moment, then charged forward.

Chuck fired at him again, but missed entirely the second time.

"Chuck!" Naomi shouted when someone grabbed her elbows from behind and pulled them back hard. She dropped the rifle.

4

"Are you all right, Mom?" Robby whispered. All the color had left his face and his eyes were wide and terrified.

She took his hand in hers and squeezed. "I'll be fine, honey," she said, her face screwed up tight. The pain was a steel band tightening around her abdomen and back

The three remaining police officers had left her and Robby where they lay and had turned their attention to the others on the floor in the gym.

"I will *not* do this!" someone shouted.

Carrie rolled onto her left side to see who was speaking. It was Mr. Iseland, one of the teachers. He stood up, tall and thin, and started walking toward the doors.

"You'll have to shoot me," he said.

One of the officers shot him twice in the back and he fell face-down and did not move again.

"Oh, Jesus," Carrie whispered. Her sense of panic clashed with the gut-wrenching pain that seemed to be wringing her body like a wet rag. "Robby, you've got to get out of here."

"How? They'll shoot me. And I can't leave you here."

There was a sound at the rear of the gymnasium and Carrie's eyes followed it. Two side doors had been opened and a man in dirty overalls stepped in. She recognized him as the school's janitor. As he stood just inside the door, a flood of burgundy flowers poured into the gymnasium, their thorny points on the hardwood floor echoing beneath the high ceiling in a kind of resonant sizzling sound.

Carrie looked around frantically until her eyes fell on one of the side entrances. It was wide open and, at the moment, no one was guarding it.

She clutched Robby's arm and whispered, "Run. You've got to run, Robby, right now. Out that door. Go."

"But Mom, I can't leave you here to—"

She squeezed his arm harder. "You don't have time to worry about me. Go get help. Run out that door. *Now*, Robby, *go!*"

He saw the seriousness in her eyes and heard it in the firmness of her pained voice. "I'll be back," he said. "I promise."

Carrie watched Robby run to the door and slip out, unseen by anyone.

As the creatures flowed over the floor toward the children like spilled liquid, screams began to fill the gymnasium.

Crushed against the floor by pain, Carrie closed her eyes a moment, wondering if this was it, her time to go, because it felt as if her strength and will and very life were gushing out onto the gymnasium floor. The screams became distant.

She opened her eyes to see a dark, blurred figure standing over her.

"You've lost a lot of blood," the figure said in a male voice that seemed to be fading. "You're no good to us."

Still fuzzy and not clearly defined, she saw him lift his arm and hold something in front of her face. When she recognized it as a gun, she thought of Robby and hoped he got away from them.

The gun fired.

5

Robby ran out of the gym and looked around. There was no one in sight. He ran around the main building to the front of the school, where he found a man getting out of a black SUV. He was covered from head to foot in a black jumpsuit with a gun in a shoulder holster and what looked like a black motorcycle helmet on his head with the black visor pulled up. He gave Robby a smile and said, "You okay?"

"My mom's in trouble," he said, breathless and fidgety. "Everybody is. They're in the gym."

"How come you're not in the gym?"

"I got away. But they're gonna come after me. My mom's hurt. She was shot."

The man nodded. "My names Jack. Who are you?"

"Robby Lodge. My mom's hurt, mister, she needs help. Are you the police?"

He smiled again. "Something like that. Tell you what, Robby. I'm on my way to see some people who can help. Get in the SUV and come with me."

"But we have to hurry, she's—"

"Don't worry, we will. Come on, get in."

Robby was nervous about getting into the SUV with the strangely dressed man, but he saw no other option. He and Jack got in, where there were two men in the back seat dressed just like Jack.

"Say hello to Robby, guys," Jack said as he started the engine. "He got away, so we're taking him with us."

6

Naomi's arms were held behind her back as she was pushed to the front of the pickup truck. Gustav did the same thing to Chuck, held his arms together behind him and pushed him forward. She did not see Donald in the crowd anymore and assumed he was the one holding her arms.

Toby and Denise and Fanny looked at them with no recognition or acknowledgment. Their faces remained expressionless.

She realized the streets were not quite as deserted as she had thought. There were people walking on the sidewalks, crossing the street. They all walked with a certain sameness—a stiffness, but also a purposefulness—and all of them seemed to be headed for the same destination—the police station. Other people were coming out of the station with handguns, shotguns, and rifles.

A black SUV sped up Main Street and stopped in front of the pickup truck. Three men got out in black jumpsuits and black helmets, and they were joined by one little boy. As the men and boy approached, he looked more and more familiar, until Naomi gasped.

"Robby? Is that you?"

Before she could get an answer, she and Chuck were turned sharply to face the Safeway they had parked in front of, where the helicopter's rotor was winding down slowly. Its hatch was open and a tall, broad-shouldered man with short blond hair walked toward them in a dark, expensive suit, eyes covered by black sunglasses. The man walked directly to Naomi and smiled, then looked around.

"Who's the boy?" he said.

One of the men from the SUV said, "His mother was shot trying to escape the gymnasium. He got away."

"Why did you bring him here? Kill him."

The man in the helmet immediately drew his gun, put it to Robby's head, and fired. The boy collapsed to the pavement.

Naomi screamed and fought the man holding her from behind. She kicked back at him and connected with his shin once. But she could not escape his hold. Instead she went limp with sobs and made him hold her up.

The man from the helicopter beckoned one of the black jumpsuits, who immediately came to his side. "How's everything working out?"

"Like a charm, sir. Unbelievably well."

Through her heartbeat pounding in her ears, Naomi heard them and straightened up a little, calming herself so she could listen.

The man smiled and nodded. "Good. In that case, you'll need to wrap things up as soon as possible. Spray the remaining flowers, round up the infested for the lab, and so we'll have something to show prospective clients, and then, uh, just clean up the mess, I guess. The roads into and out of town are blocked and we've got a few stories going out, enough to confuse everyone. First, it'll be a chemical spill, or something, requiring the closing of the roads, and then, no, it's a terrorist attack and most of the town has been wiped out. Nobody'll know what the hell is going on for a while, but they'll settle for terrorist attack. Soon as we've got everything we need, we'll flame a big chunk of the town and be on our way."

The helpless surrender Naomi had felt only a moment ago was swept away by a fierce and sudden anger when she heard the man's words. She remained limp in the arms of the man holding her, listening. Limp enough so that his hold on her was not as firm as before.

"Will do, sir," the black jumpsuit said. "Anything else?"

"I'll see you in my office at nine tomorrow morning with a full and detailed report on the project. And I want to know how soon we can make this available to our clients."

When Naomi closed her eyes, all she could see was Robby being shot in the head at point-blank range and dropping to the ground like a puppet whose strings had suddenly been cut. She was afraid she would be seeing that for a long time and suddenly her anger was a sick knot in her stomach that she could hold in no longer.

With all her strength, Naomi suddenly launched herself away from the man, wrenched her arms out of his grip, and lunged at the man from the helicopter, arms outstretched, fingers curved as she screamed.

The man reared back, stumbled backward, and tried to avoid her, but she kept coming until she was on him, her fingernails clawing his face as her rage reduced her screams to gibberish. He tried to grab her arms, but she was too frantic and animated.

The black jumpsuit stepped forward and was joined by a couple of others in pulling her away from the man from the helicopter.

The man touched his face cautiously, then checked his fingers. He was bleeding. "Dammit," he muttered. Then he looked at Naomi, glanced at Chuck, then back at Naomi. "Who are these people?" he said without taking his eyes from her.

Someone said, "They just drove up and started shooting."

To the black jumpsuit, the man from the helicopter said, "You heard everything I told you?"

"Every word."

"Good." He nodded toward Naomi. "Kill them." Then he turned and headed back toward the helicopter.

Naomi suddenly felt all her energy drain out of her and she fell back against the man holding her. As one of the black jumpsuits came toward her, drawing his gun, she tried to turn so she could see Chuck. She tried to call his name but her throat was dry and coarse and her voice was nothing but a whisper.

Then the gun was in her face, and the world exploded into nothingness.

Chapter Seven

Alice paced as she drank her wine and peripherally watched the news on TV. She had opened the last bottle of red in the house, a cabernet that was not very good, but she hardly tasted it, anyway, because she was so worried about Carrie and Robby. Carrie had told her on the phone that she would be leaving the diner to pick up Robby and they would come straight home. That had been more than ninety minutes ago. Alice got no answer when she called Carrie's cell phone, not even the usual recording of Carrie asking her to leave a message, and there was no answer at the diner.

Then the game show she had been watching was interrupted by a news bulletin announcing that all roads into and out of Mount Crag were closed due to a spill of some kind. There was video of cars being turned away, forced to turn around and drive away from Mount Crag. The details were sketchy, but authorities asked that locals stay indoors.

It made no sense to Alice. If it was a toxic spill, why did they close the roads going in both directions? The spill could not be on both sides of town. But what did she know? She was a drunk sixty-eight-year-old college dropout who was too busy worrying about her daughter and grandson to pay much attention to the fact that there definitely was something fishy about the road closings and the spill, or whatever it was.

Alice kept thinking, *It's something bad and they're gonna cover it up.*

She finished the cabernet and went to the kitchen, dropped the empty bottle and its cork into the garbage can at the end of the counter, rinsed her wine glass, and put it on the wooden dish rack to dry. She opened a dry chardonnay, dropped a few ice cubes into a tall water glass, and filled it up. It would be nice if it could chill in the fridge for a couple of hours, but Alice Lodge was not a proud woman, especially when she was so worried.

In the living room, she flopped into the recliner facing the TV and changed the station to one of the few daytime soap operas still on network TV. She hoped that would distract her from repeatedly calling Carrie's phone or the diner.

Alice drank her wine, watched her show, got up and paced a while, drink in hand, sat down, and watched TV again for a while. She repeated this process until, pacing in the living room, she looked out the front window and something caught her eye. Something small, scrambling across the front lawn. She stopped pacing and peered out the window as another one darted over the grass. And another. There was one on the sidewalk, and another scurrying over the pavement in the street. They were flowers. Those strange flowers that had appeared that morning. But they were skittering around like crabs or spiders.

She took a moment to ask herself if she was hallucinating. Alice was terrified of learning she had some kind of mind-destroying disease like dementia or Alzheimer's, and sometimes she checked herself, just to make sure she was not going crazy. This was one of those times because skittering flowers made no sense. She emptied her glass, set it on the small table beside the recliner, and closed the drapes so she would not have to wonder about what those things might be. Then she went to the kitchen for a refill.

When she returned, she dropped into the recliner again and sipped her wine as she watched whatever was on the TV screen. Before she could figure out what that was, Alice drifted off to sleep.

The trilling of the telephone woke her and she answered hoarsely. A moment later, she said, "No, I do *not* want a reverse mortgage." She thumbed the OFF button on the cordless landline and placed it back on the small table beside her drink, picked up her drink and took several healthy swallows.

When she looked at the TV screen, she saw the cars still being turned away by police outside of Mount Crag. But she had turned on a soap opera. This was the network news, she realized, and the inside of her chest felt cold when she read the words at the bottom of the screen: TERRORIST ATTACK?

What? A terrorist attack in Mount Crag? She fumbled with the remote and turned up the volume.

The concerned anchorman said, "Once again, nothing is known for certain as yet."

"When did *that* ever stop you?" Alice snapped.

"There appears to be a lot of smoke rising from the area of Mount Crag, the town proper, but communication has been —"

The TV blinked out and the lights went off.

"Shit," she said, standing. She immediately dropped back into the chair as a wave of dizziness spun the room around her. She grabbed her glass, tipped it up to her mouth and emptied it, then stood slowly. She stood in the dark living room for a moment, then went to the window and opened the drapes, letting in the day's gray light.

A large, black SUV drove slowly by the house with two men walking in front of it and two behind. The men in the black jumpsuits and helmets each held a hose attached to the tank on his back and sprayed a thin, steady mist into the air as he walked.

Alice did not understand it, and she certainly did not like it. Something about it filled her with dread, made her afraid to know exactly what it was they were doing out there.

She took her glass to the kitchen for more wine, but first she went down the hall to her bedroom, swaying a bit on the way, and found her portable radio. It operated on batteries, which were already in it. In the kitchen, she placed the radio on the counter and found the news/talk station.

"—if it was terrorism or if it *wasn't* terrorism, I want to be clear about that, no matter how many times I have to say it, we really do not know what's happened in Mount Crag, but judging by the amount of smoke, it's bad."

Smoke? Alice dropped a few more ice cubes in her glass, finished off the bottle of chardonnay and opened another, topped off her glass, and carried it back to the living room with the radio. She put them both on the table by the phone and went to the window again. The SUV and the men in black with their spraying hoses were gone. Had they really been there? She saw no smoke, no chaos. What was the man on the radio talking about?

Alice paced for a while, then picked up the phone. She called Carrie's phone and got no answer, then the diner, and got no answer. An overwhelming urge to cry suddenly hit her, but all she did was whimper. She put the phone down, returned to the chair, and held her drink. She stared at the dead TV screen, listened to the radio, and waited.

That was what she would do, she decided. Surely Carrie and Robby would arrive with a frantic story about what took them so long. Or Carrie would call. Or someone would call. Or come. Something *had* to happen.

Alice took a couple of swallows of wine, wiggled herself into a comfortably settled position in the recliner, and waited.

About the Author

Ray Garton has been writing novels, novellas, short stories, and essays for more than 30 years. His work spans the genres of horror, crime, suspense, and even comedy. *Live Girls* was nominated for the Bram Stoker Award in 1988, and Garton received the Grand Master of Horror Award at the 2006 World Horror Convention. He lives in northern California with his wife Dawn, where he is at work on a new novel.

BIBLIOGRAPHY

NOVELS AND NOVELLAS

411
Bestial
Biofire
Crawlers
Crucifax
Dark Channel

Darklings
Live Girls
Lot Lizards
Loveless
Night Life
Meds
Murder Was My Alibi
Ravenous
Scissors
Seductions
Serpent Girl
Sex and Violence in Hollywood
Shackled
The Folks
The Folks 2
The Loveliest Dead
The Man in the Palace Theater
The New Neighbor
Trade Secrets
Trailer Park Noir
Vortex
Zombie Love

COLLECTIONS
Methods of Madness
'Nids And Other Stories
Pieces of Hate
Slivers of Bone
The Disappeared and Other Stories
The Girl in the Basement and Other Stories
Wailing and Gnashing of Teeth

Curious about other Crossroad Press books? Stop by our
website: http://crossroadpress.com
We offer quality writing
in digital, audio, and print formats.

Subscribe to our newsletter on the website homepage and
receive a free eBook.